Timmy in the clink? That's going to cramp his style a bit, isn't it?
Well, not really – not with a prisoner of Timmy's imagination.
Especially when the clink in question is a liberal-minded open prison – and Timmy discovers just how open that can be! Even more so with visitors like Daisy Deacon and warders' wives like Mrs Sinden. And when his varied experiences of life on the outside qualify our hero to sit on the board of a pornography commission, life in the clink reveals new vistas of fact-finding fun for Timmy.

Also by Timothy Lea and available from Sphere Books

- CONFESSIONS OF A WINDOW CLEANER
- CONFESSIONS OF A DRIVING INSTRUCTOR
- CONFESSIONS FROM A HOLIDAY CAMP
- CONFESSIONS FROM A HOTEL
- CONFESSIONS OF A TRAVELLING SALESMAN
- CONFESSIONS OF A FILM EXTRA

Confessions from the Clink

TIMOTHY LEA

SPHERE BOOKS LIMITED
30/32 Gray's Inn Road, London WC1X 8JL

First published in Great Britain
by Sphere Books Ltd 1973

Reprinted February 1974
Reprinted July 1974
Reprinted August 1974

TRADE
MARK

Set in Linotype Baskerville

Printed in Great Britain by
Hazell Watson & Viney Ltd
Aylesbury, Bucks

ISBN 0 7221 9321 1

Contents

CHAPTER ONE

Twelve months in the nick! I could hardly believe my jug handles when the beak passed sentence. It looked as if it was all he could pass, too. I have never seen a more tight-lipped, prune-featured old git. And all for having a few magic moments of hampton parking immortalised on celluloid. Talk about diabolical! I have never known such a travesty of British justice since they put me away for nicking lead – at the time I thought I was taking part in a slum clearance scheme. It is not as if I wanted to flash my nasty at the great British public either. A few innocent recreational moments with a bevy of fun-loving Cypriot ladies were not meant to be shown as family entertainment. How I came to be blamed because some berk cuts them into the final version of 'Revenge of the Creature from the O.K. Corral' is beyond me. Likewise, how I became responsible for the whole film. I thought it was a Trion Production promoted by Justin Tymeley and my brother-in-law, Sidney, but it just goes to show how wrong you can be.

"Terribly unlucky, Timmy boy," says Sid when he comes to visit me in my cell. "I feel very guilty about this. I wanted to give you a fair crack of the whip, that's all."

"So did that old bleeder on the bench," I yelp. "He said he was sorry he couldn't give me the cat."

"I know," says Sidney, shaking his head. "They shouldn't allow them to say things like that. He's past it, that bloke."

"He's passed it alright. Twelve bleeding months. Do you think I should appeal?"

Sid shakes his head again. "I've spoken to Mr. Rampersand and he's definitely against it. He said they're very hot on pornography at the moment and you might get another six months."

"Gordon Bennett! I'm innocent. How come you and Justin weren't up there with me? That's what I can't understand."

Sidney extends his arms despairingly. "Like I said, Timmo. I was just trying to put a bit of moola your way. You've always said to me that you never had a real stake in any of our ventures so I thought I'd remedy that this time."

"Very considerate, Sidney."

"I'm glad you see it that way."

"So that piece of paper I signed made me responsible for all the company's liabilities?"

"That kind of thing, Timmy. I don't want to confuse you with a lot of technical details at a moment like this."

"Don't worry about that, Sidney. It will give me something to think about in the next twelve months. I suppose my responsibilities don't extend to control of the profits?"

"No, Timmo. You see, it wouldn't be practical with you in the chokey, would it? Don't worry. There's a good reason for doing things the way we are."

"Yes, Sid. I think I know what it is: sheer, naked greed. You've made me the fall guy so that you and Justin can grab all the loot."

"Timmo!" If you didn't know Sidney, you would think he was really hurt. "That's a terrible thing to say."

"It's bleeding true, though. Even with my bit cut out, that film is going to make a million. The publicity has been fantastic."

"Don't worry, Timmo. We'll see you all right. Justin has got a lot of influence in the prison world."

"That doesn't surprise me."

"No bitterness, Timmo. It's unworthy of you. What I was saying is that Justin is trying to pull a few strings to make sure you get sent to a nice nick. Once they've made an example of you, they don't want to lay it on too thick."

"Very kind of them."

"Penhurst. Have you heard of it?"

"Not unless it's in the Good Food Guide."

"It's a very enlightened place. You get a nice class of person there."

"That's always important, isn't it? I don't want to mix with a lot of rubbish."

Sidney shakes his head. "You're very difficult to help, sometimes, Timmo. Justin has gone to a lot of trouble on your behalf."

It is at this point that I begin to see more red than if I had my mug pressed against a baboon's bum. *"Justin has gone to a lot of trouble!"* I yelp. "What about me?! Twelve months in the chokey. What's going to happen to my sex life?"

"Well, you'll have to cut down a bit."

" 'A bit'! You must be joking."

"I expect you'll get some remission."

"Quite a few of them, I should reckon. I can see my wrists in plaster by the time I get out."

"I meant that they'll probably lop a bit off your sentence for good behaviour," says Sid huffily. "There's no need to be coarse."

"They might as well lop a bit off my old man. I'm never going to last for twelve months without crumpet."

"We'll send you food parcels."

"Food parcels? You'd be better off sending me a vat of bromide."

I mean, it is disturbing, isn't it? It can't be good for my action man kit to be put in cold storage for a year. I am one of those blokes who needs it fairly regularly to keep in trim. You can't deny a great artist the use of his paint brush for twelve months and then expect him to bash out the Mona Lisa, can you? "What about Mum and Dad?" I say, deciding that I do not want to think about my fast fading sex life any longer.

"She's loyal, your mum," says Sid. "A diabolical cook, but loyal. She reckoned it was because you had that coloured fellow that you got put away."

"You mean my solicitor, Rampersand?"

"That's him. Mum said she could see that the judge

was going to have no truck with him. I think she might have a point there. The miserable basket started looking old-fashioned the minute Rumpleknickers made you take the oath on those crossed chicken bones."

"Well, it was his first case in an English Court, wasn't it?"

"I know, but you'd think he would check up, wouldn't you? I mean, when he started throwing that white powder about and flapping his fly whisk, I could see the jury was going off him. No, on reflection, I think your mother was dead right."

"What about Dad? I haven't seen him tripping down those stairs."

"Well, you wouldn't, would you? Probably scared of seeing too many old friends. He's very distressed about the whole thing. Says he can't hold his head up in the Highwayman any more."

"Give him a couple of beers and he has trouble holding his head up anywhere. I don't know what he's going on about. He's one of the reasons why I'm stuck in this place." This is indeed true and comes about from the fact that dad's porn collection, concealed in the hallstand, was considered to be mine by the searching 'bules. Fresh evidence of my depraved nature. In fact, though never averse to a quick butchers, I would rather spend my money on the real thing.

Dad works, for want of a better word, at the Lost Property Office and is swift to fall upon those articles which nobody would ever have the face to claim. Blood supposedly being thicker than water you would have thought that he might have stepped forward to acknowledge ownership of "Wife-Swapping – Danish Style" and "Spanking for Beginners", but not a sausage. He allows his firstborn to be put away without a murmur.

Sid sticks a hand through the bars and pats me on the shoulder. "I know, Timmy. Your dad has behaved rotten, but don't worry. I'll stand by you. I'll send you a postcard."

"Where from?" I say, allowing a trace of bitterness to creep into my voice.

"The last few weeks have been a big strain, Timmy. I thought I'd take Rosie and the kids for a bit of sunshine. Sardinia has been recommended to me."

"Oh, that's blooming marvellous, isn't it? I go in the nick and you go off to Sardinia. There's no justice."

It is shortly after this exchange that Sidney goes up the steps from the cells nursing a thick lip and I find myself lumbered with a swollen knuckle that prevents me succumbing immediately to a spot of percy pummelling.

The next day I hear that, either by luck or design, I am being sent to Penhurst Prison and it is clearly a decision that causes resentment amongst my 'bule friends.

"Place is a blinking holiday camp," snorts one of them. "You want to take your tennis racquet."

"And your camera," says another. "Or maybe not, knowing the kind of pictures you like taking."

I don't argue the toss but climb aboard the H.M. Prisons van which I share with a pasty-faced bloke with two-tone hair. The first half inch is black and the rest yellow.

"Ooh!" he says, pursing his lips at me. "Thank goodness for a little company at least. What naughty things have you been up to?" It occurs to me without too much effort that this bloke is never going to be a serious threat to George Foreman but it is an impression I keep to myself. It takes all sorts to make licquorice, as my old school master used to say.

"It's a very long and turgid story," I tell him, "but basically they got me for making and appearing in blue films."

"Ooh! That must be difficult," says my new friend. "I suppose you set up the camera, run out and do your bit, and run back again. Must be very tiring."

"I wasn't doing both at the same time," I explain. "In fact, I didn't know I was being filmed."

"Ooh, that is treacherous. Taking advantage of someone like that. It's not right, is it? But, you know –" Streaky squeezes my arm conspiratorially – "I'm surprised they were able to recognise you. Some of those films. I mean, really. People know me by my face. The way they go on about it, you wouldn't recognise your own mother. I know, because she was in one. Marvellous woman. She'd bend over backwards to help a complete stranger. That was her trouble really. She was just too – you know what I mean?"

"Er – yes," I say. "Heart as big as all outdoors."

"Not only her heart, ducky. She was a lot of woman in more ways than one. Quite overpowering, in fact."

I have a shrewd idea that Two-Tone Jessie O'Gay is not in clink for tying parking meters in knots, and he is quick to reinforce this impression.

"It's disgraceful me being in here, too. I mean, when a cute blonde number comes up to you in the little boys' room and says 'hello sailor' you don't expect him to be playing scrum-half for the Metropolitan Police Rugby Team, do you? I was quite overcome. Over, I have never been so come."

"Diabolical," I say. "I know just how you feel. I mean –" I add hurriedly, "It's not on, is it?"

"Oh, you are nice," says Streaky, giving me another little squeeze. "I said to myself the moment I saw you. 'He's nice,' I said. I'm so glad we met up. We'll be able to stick together, won't we?"

I think the answer to that must be no, but I don't want to give offence too early in our non-relationship. "My name's Timothy Lea," I say, trying to sound as if I can strip paint by huffing on it.

"Fran Warren," says my adorable comrade. "Fran, short for Francis, but long for everyone else. Oops, sorry. Just my little joke."

A few more like that and I will have committed murder before we ever get to the nick, I think to myself. What a laugh riot this little number is turning out to be.

"It would be nice if we could share, though, wouldn't it?" warbles Mrs. Warren's problem child. "I'm certain we'd get on well. I mean, you must be broad-minded."

"Exactly," I said hurriedly. "That's all my mind ever thinks about – broads."

"Ooh, you're like that, are you?" He manages to make it sound as if I enjoy interfering with garden gnomes.

"Birds," I say firmly. "I love 'em. That's my scene. Birds, lots of birds. And football. Chelsea. We are the champions! We are the –!"

"Yes, all right, dear," says Fran holding up his hands in dismay. "There's no need to shout. We all have our little idiosyncrasies. I support Norwich City, myself. That heavenly yellow. And their goalkeeper! He's a dream. Like a big pussy cat throwing himself all over the place. Ooh, I feel like standing in the way every time I see him."

I do not think a common interest in football is going to be enough to make life with Francis Warren bearable. Certainly not when my interest is nowhere near half as common as his.

I hope they are not all going to be like him at Penhurst. Of course, I have heard stories – and it is not surprising when the crumpet ration is akin to the number of nips rolling up to a Kamikazi pilots reunion dinner – but I did not expect to get lumbered before I got through the front gate.

This article presents itself before I have had to slap my companion's wrist more than a couple of times, and bears a stronger resemblance to the entrance to a crematorium than a nick – with my family you get plenty of chance to see both. There is a bloke in a peaked cap behind the wrought iron gate and the minute I see him, I am reminded of the Funfrall Holiday Camp I once worked at. I hope the nosh is better here.

The driver's neck, seen through the glass panel behind his seat, looks like a pink elephant sitting down, and I turn away from it to feast my eyes on Fran plucking at his disgusting hair.

"Oh, it's awful, isn't it?" he squeaks. "I saw you looking. I've got split ends and my follicles are clogged."

Please! I feel like saying to him. Spare me the details! I mean, there are some things you just don't want to know about, aren't there? "I was on remand for three weeks," he clucks, "never had a chance to do anything about it."

"Don't worry," I soothe. "I'm certain they'll make allowances."

"O.K. you two. Out!" The prison officer swings open the door and divides his contempt between us. I am not certain I like the way he says "you two" as if we were some kind of double act.

"Oh dear. What a shame. Just as we were getting down to brass tacks, too. It's always the same, isn't it?" I ignore the bent gent's twitter and step down to take a butcher's at the scenery. The building we are outside looks like a modern country house with two wings and a front bit that has more windows than a Peeping Tom's training camp. They all have bars across them but apart from that, there is nothing that shouts "nick" too crudely. There is even a football pitch in the middle of the ample grounds.

"Right. Up the steps and report to reception. The Governor will want to see you."

"Ooh. Aren't you going to carry my bag?" sniffs Fran.

"I wouldn't trust myself to bend down and pick it up," says the screw. "Now hop it." He slams the door and climbs back into the driver's seat.

"Charming!" says Fran. "No room service and nobody to meet us. I wonder they didn't make us walk from the gate. I'm not certain I'm going to like it here. The vibrations aren't right. Do you ever feel like that? Maybe I'm over-sensitive. I had a friend once who –"

"Yeah, yeah," I say, before he can get into full spate. "We'd better do like the man says, hadn't we?" I nip up the steps and push open the door that is already ajar.

Inside, a tall bloke in blue shirt and denims is counting

a roll of greasy one pound notes. He stops when he sees us and looks us up and down suspiciously.

"We're looking for the Governor," I say.

"Oh yeah. New boys, are you?"

We nod.

"Welcome to Sinnerama Holiday. Follow me. I think he's free at the moment."

"Is it nice here?" twitters Fran.

"It's bleeding lovely, mate," says our guide. "You two together, are you?"

"Yes."

"No!" I yelp. "We came together, that's all."

"That's all?" trills Fran. "Don't knock it, ducky!" Before he can pursue the subject further our guide taps respectfully on one of the doors and a voice that sounds like two pieces of sand paper having it away bids us enter.

The inside of the room surprises me. I had not been expecting the state apartment at Windsor Castle but certainly something a bit more flash than this. The Playboy Calendar on the wall strikes an odd note, too. What is most unexpected is that there are bars on the windows. I puzzle about this for a minute before it occurs to me that they probably have some deep psychological significance. Maybe it helps the inmates to identify with the governor if he gives the appearance of living under the same conditions as they do. Fascinating, isn't it? Oh well, please yourselves.

"Two new boys, governor," says our guide, waving us forward.

"Thanks, Grass," rasps the figure behind the desk. "Harvest coming in all right?"

"Fantastic. We've almost got more than we can process."

"Excellent. Excellent. Don't let me hold you up, then."

Our guide withdraws and I concentrate on the governor. He is a large, squarely-built man with a couple of days' growth of stubble and tattoos going right up his arms. He, too, is wearing a blue denim shirt with rolled up sleeves so it is easy to see the artwork. "Mum, I love you" says one arm. "Per ardua ad astra" says the other. A nice combination of the sentimental and the intellectual, I think to myself. Very rounded personality, obviously. I never thought that a nick would go to the trouble of making it so easy for the prisoners to identify with their surroundings. Fancy, even dressing the governor up like one of the inmates. Maybe life is better under the Conservatives.

"Hello, boys," says the governor cheerfully. "Fancy a drink, do you? I've got a nice drop of Spanish Burgundy here, or how about Bristol Cream?"

"Ooh, I thought you said Bristol queen for a moment," squeaks Fran. "You almost offended me. I come from Bristol, you know. It's a rough, manly town absolutely bursting at the seams with Jolly Jack Tars."

"Hello, sailor," says the governor. "Who's your shipmate?"

"We'd never seen each other before today," I yelp. Blimey, if this goes on I'll have to get a placard printed.

"Two orphans of the storm whom fate has thrown together," simpers Fran. "Will we be sharing a cell?"

"No! No!" I shout before the governor can say anything. "I have these terrible nightmares when I start lashing out at anything that stands in my path. I can be uncontrollably violent. I wouldn't ask anybody to risk that."

"Ooh," says Fran, "I'm a great soother. I bet you, if I massage your temples every night before –"

"No!"

"Ooh, you're such a spoilsport. I know you want to, really."

"Yeah, yeah," says the governor, waving at Fran to belt up. "If you've got any complaints about the accommodation we'll sort those out later. The Domestic Affairs Committee will deal with it. Now, what are you two boys in for?"

While we tell him and sip our drinks it occurs to me

that it is strange that he does not know already. This must be a very free and easy place if prisoners can roll up unannounced. Maybe a lot of them escape too, so that it is difficult to keep track of numbers.

"Do you have a large turnover?" I ask.

"About two hundred thou at the moment," says our genial governor helping himself to a generous slug of sherry. "But we're pushing it up fast."

"Two hundred thousand prisoners?" I gasp.

"Two hundred thousand nicker, you berk," croaks the governor. "Blimey, you're as green as the blokes what are supposed to be running this place."

While I ponder that remark, the door opens and a tall pinched geezer comes in. He has watery eyes and a face so thin that you feel he must have caught his nut between a couple of mating elephants. What strikes me most about him is his clobber. He is wearing a navy blue tunic with silver buttons and two pips on the epaulettes. It is a bit dressy for this establishment and, of course, dead out of fashion. His best friend should tell him.

"Legend!"

"Yes, Governor?"

Are my ears deceiving me? Our tattooed friend behind the desk is addressing the newcomer as *Governor*. There must be some mistake.

"There must be some mistake, Legend." The tone suggests that the speaker might burst into tears at any minute. "All prisoners – I mean, all residents reporting to the House are supposed to report to me before they go to their rooms."

The man addressed as Legend claps his hands to his head dramatically and jumps to his feet.

"Governor! I had no idea. Oh dear. This is awful. I can see how put out you must be. Otherwise you would never have used that nasty word."

"Yes. Yes," splutters the new governor. "I'm sorry about that. I don't know what came over me."

Legend holds up his hand. "Don't say another word,

Governor. We all slip up sometimes. I suppose that is why a lot of us are here." He says it so that you expect to see a halo come sprouting out of his bonce.

"Of course, of course." The Governor seems embarrassed. "I'm sorry I burst out like that. It was unforgivable of me."

"Don't worry about it, Governor. We forgive you, don't we lads? Life has taught us how to turn the other cheek." We nod vigorously. "Now, go along with the Governor, lads. He's a man we all respect. He'll see you all right. You haven't got time for a glass of sherry before you go, Governor?"

"Regrettably not, Legend," says wafer-bonce, looking as if his moist eyes are going to start melting down his cheeks at any minute. "By the way, how is the spinach coming along?"

Legend's wizened mug twinkles like the inside of an empty whelk shell.

"Excellent, Governor, excellent. We're very grateful for that manure you provided. It makes all the difference."

"And you've had no difficulty in finding someone to take it off your hands?"

"No. Soap and water seems to work all right if you scrub long enough."

"I meant the spinach," says the Governor patiently.

"Oh! That. No, Governor, no. Of course, the price isn't all it could be, but I think it will get better when we can put more on the market."

"So you're going to be a spinach baron, are you, Legend?"

Legend laughs uproariously at the joke. "Oh, no, Governor. Nothing like that. As long as we can scrape up enough to buy the lads a few little creature comforts, that's all I'm interested in."

"Capital, Legend. Capital. Your initiative and fellow-feeling do you much credit." As Legend lowers his eyes humbly to the floor the Governor turns to us. "When I look at what's happening in the world outside, I sometimes ask myself if the right men are behind bars."

I think I could help him answer that one, but my natural sense of self-preservation keeps my cakehole firmly closed. Legend looks like a dab hand at instant plastic surgery. We leave him waving a couple of fingers at the Governor's back and follow that gentleman down a long corridor and out into a courtyard which gives access to another part of the "Complex" as the Governor chooses to call it. On the way he is rabbiting about "behavioural patterns", "individual freedoms" "society's responsibility to the under-privileged" and all that stuff you get on the telly when everyone has gone to bed, but I am not listening. I am watching the bird who has come willowing out of one of the doors on the other side of the courtyard. The fact that she is a bird and not a bloke is pretty impressive to start off with, but her own natural advantages would win wolf whistles in any company. Even with her hair in curlers and struggling under the weight of a plastic dustbin she is still mucho woman. I rush forward just as she is starting to lose a high-heeled carpet slipper and clap my mitts on the dustbin. "Allow me," I husk, giving her a look of smouldering passion calculated to perish the elastic in her knickers, should she be wearing any. "Where would you like me to put it?"

She holds my glance and as our eyes fuse across the top of the empty Kit-E-Kat tins, I think that this could be the start of something very beautiful.

"Over there," she says and with that suppleness of movement that so characterises the Leas, I step backwards, trip over something and sit down emptying half a ton of fish-heads into my lap. It is not done in a way that would make Cary Grant envious and I sense that a magic moment has escaped for ever.

"She looked a brazen bit, that one," sniffs Fran as we go on our way. "I didn't think there'd be any of her type here."

"That's Mrs. Sinden," says the Governor, whose name

is Brownjob – diabolically bad luck, isn't it? – "She's married to one of the-er guardians."
"You mean warders?" says Fran.
Brownjob winces. "We call them guardians, here, Warren. Our whole aim is to build a bridge between our community and the outside world. We want to avoid the creation of a convict mentality that cannot make its way in normal society. We eschew words like 'prison', 'warder' and 'cell'. You have a 'room' in a 'house' and are looked after by 'guardians' who are there to help you. As much as possible we try to create an environment in which the house can be run by 'the guests' – or yourselves. We have committees who operate in different areas and are composed of guests with a leavening of guardians to act as mediators should there be a divergence of opinions."
I don't understand everything he is rabbiting about but I can understand why the rozzers thought that Penhurst was a doddle. What a carve up! Brownjob spouting all that balls whilst Legend and his lads are making two hundred thousand quid flogging spinach. There must be a fantastic amount of it to earn that kind of money. Or maybe they do other things as well? They must do, if Legend reckons that they are going to expand as fast as he indicated.
To my relief, Brownjob explains that we will have individual rooms and adds, apologetically, that they will be locked at ten o'clock each night. I am dead relieved to hear it because I do not fancy Mrs. Warren's little boy trying to massage my temples every evening. Without protection I might be tempted to respond with half a brick. We also learn that we are being allocated to a job and that I am being sent to help in the Prison laundry.
"The irony will not be lost on you," chortles Brownjob as I stare at him stonily to prove it is.
Meals are self-service and eaten in a large airy cafeteria and I am amazed at how good the nosh is. I wish mum could come here to pick up a few lessons. Just to think of

her cooking makes me see the label on a tube of Rennies.

Warren follows me around like I have him on a piece of string and I can see the two of us getting a few old-fashioned glances from the rest of the inmates.

"Hello, sailor," says Legend every time he sees one of us and I am most distressed that he reckons me to be one half of a set of poofters.

The thought is much on my mind then next morning when I find myself despatched to collect dirty laundry from the "guardians'" quarters. It has now been a matter of weeks since Percy last found gainful employment and to say that I am feeling frustrated is rather like describing Yul Brynner's hairline as receding. Even Fran Warren is beginning to look like Shirley Temple and if I don't do something fast I could be in more trouble than an octopus with smelly armpits.

I give a sharp rat-tat-tat on Mrs. Sinden's door and look forward to the sight of a one-hundred-per-cent-red-blooded woman. In such cases it is usually my fortune to find her old man at home with flu, or half a dozen kids struggling on the doormat but this time the delectable crumpet factory flings open the door, to all intents and purposes, on her tod.

"Oh," she says. "You've come to empty the dustbins, have you?"

I don't say anything because I am concentrating on her cleavage which looks deeper than a fisherman's wader. No obstacle obstructs my peepers because her frilly housecoat sweeps across her bristols at nipple height.

"Er, no," I gulp. "It's your laundry I'm after."

"Oh, dear," she says. "I'd forgotten it was Wednesday. You'd better come in while I sort some out. Do you fancy a cup of tea?"

"That would be very nice, if you can spare the time," I say.

"No trouble at all. Come in."

I am across the threshold before you can say "Bring back the Cat" or "Pussy Galore" as Ian Fleming has it.

"I'm not certain I should let you in," she says archly as I settle myself down before a packet of Wonder Wheaties "the cereal that put men on the moon".

"You mean because I'm a – a guest?" I say. "I feel such a berk using that word."

"Because of what you're here for," says Mrs. S. waggling her fingers at me roguishly. "I know, you know. My hubby told me all about it."

It is indeed amazing how quickly details of my "crime" seem to have spread round the camp and I have been aware of a good deal of "nudge, nudge, wink, wink" dogging my petal footsteps ever since I left Brownjob's office. This, coupled to the attention of the dreary Fran has made me feel about as inconspicuous as Sammy Davis Junior at a Klu Klux Klan rally.

"Oh. That," I say studying the small print on the back of the Wheaties packet: "build your own spacecraft. Unbelievable offer. No experience necessary. All you need is a screwdriver. Hours of good, clean fun for all the family".

"Yes, that," she says eagerly. "You're a naughty boy, aren't you? I'd never have thought it to look at you."

"Still waters run deep," I say giving her the old smoulder.

"I don't think I want to let you see my smalls."

"Depends whether you're in them or not, doesn't it?"

"Cheeky!"

In her case the word "smalls" is blooming ridiculous. I look at her cleavage and go weak at the knees. How much is a man supposed not to take?

"I'd better empty the laundry basket," she says. "Make yourself at home."

She swings out of the room and I gulp down my tea and wonder what to do next. It is always a bit tricky, this. Follow her upstairs and I could be accused of rushing things. Sit where I am and she probably reckons I don't fancy it. What would you do? Jot down your answer on the back of a five quid note and – no, don't bother. There isn't time. I know! I leap to my feet and trot to the bottom of the stairs.

"Can I use the toilet?" I holler.

Not the most romantic invitation to a nooky carnival, but it does sound more convincing than asking if she would like to see my stag beetle.

"First on the right at the top of the stairs," she shouts. "I've got something to show you when you come down."

I am getting so excited in the khasi that I have to be very careful not to spoil the décor. What has Mrs. Sinden got to show me that I have not nearly clotted my sporran on already? I pull the chain and race downstairs reckoning that if I get to the bottom before it reaches its crescendo a spot of in and out with Mrs. S. is a certainty. I used to do the same when I was a kid only then my end was slightly different – slightly smaller, too.

"What do you think of this?" says Mrs. S. coyly as I slink into the kitchen.

I tear my eyes away from her boobs and focus on the photograph she has handed me. By the cringe! It is none other than her lovely self in a state of undress I can only describe as stark naked. It is not a very good photograph but there is no mistaking our girl's best features.

"Very nice," I say. "A bit over-exposed, but – er very nice. When did you have this done?"

"About two months ago. I had a whole lot done. That was the best one. Though the smile's a bit unnatural, isn't it?"

I reckon my smile would be a bit unnatural if I was a tart standing naked with a loaf of French bread between my legs, but I don't say anything.

"I sent them up to 'Bedside Winkie', but they didn't publish them," continues Mrs. S. "I got a very strange letter from a man who said he wanted to retouch my originals."

"I know just how he felt," I husk. "Who took them?"

Mrs. S. blushes and fiddles with her hair. "One of my

husband's friends. He got a photograph in the 'Royston Crow' once."

"Not one of these?"

"Oh no. It was of a couple of pumpkins."

Not so blooming different, I think to myself.

"What does your husband think of them?" I ask.

"He hasn't seen them. He's a bit old-fashioned. I wouldn't want him to be upset."

Thoughtful, isn't she? I do like that in a woman – amongst other things. It occurs to me that Mrs. S. is referring herself to me in a professional capacity, obviously reckoning that a man in my line of business must be able to recognise a couple, or three, of good things when he sees them. I am not slow to act upon this thought.

"You've certainly got tremendous potential," I say, seriously. "I just wonder if it has been properly exploited."

"What do you mean?" Mrs. S. cranes forward eagerly and it is like peeping over the edge of the Grand Canyon to gaze down between her tits.

"Well, of course, I've had a bit of experience of this kind of thing and –"

" 'A bit!' "

I smile modestly. "I'd say his equipment wasn't up to scratch."

"There was nothing wrong with his equipment," says Mrs. S. firmly. "I'll vouch for that."

"Must have been the lighting, then. He was flashing, was he?"

"Just to start with."

"U-m-m-m. What a pity we're not in my studio at the moment. I could show you what I meant. Maybe when I get out."

Mrs. S. leans forward again and I have to avert my eyes.

"Oh yes. That would be marvellous. I'd be ever so grateful."

"You're very keen, aren't you?"

"Well, you get fed up with doing the same thing all your life, don't you? Being a warder's – I mean – guardian's wife, isn't much to write home about. I long for a change sometimes. And I've always reckoned I'm as good as those girls you see in the papers."

"Better."

"Are you serious?"

"Very. Of course, I can't be absolutely certain when you've got that thing on." I smother a non-existent yawn to show that my interest is on the level.

"Would you – would you be prepared to give me your professional opinion?"

I pretend to give the matter serious thought.

"I don't know if I should, really," I say eventually. "I mean, your husband probably wouldn't like it."

"He won't know. He's picking up a new intake from town."

Boy, oh boy! When Percy hears that, he is jumping up and down the front of my jeans like a restless bull mastiff being told it is walkies time.

"We'd better go upstairs," I say, a shade too hurriedly. "The light's not so good down here."

She leads the way and I can hardly keep my hand on the bannister.

"I'm afraid the bedroom is a bit of a mess," she says. "You'll have to forgive me."

"I won't look," I say skittishly.

"Of course, I know I've put on a bit of weight since those photos were taken. I can get that off again if you think I've got the potential."

You've got the potential all right, darling, I think to myself. Lots and lots of it.

"Shall I do some poses?" says Mrs. S. eagerly.

Why not? In fact, what a good idea.

"Yes, you do your stuff and I'll see if I can make any suggestions."

Mrs. S. takes a deep breath – and with those knockers

the breaths have to be deep, believe me, and wriggles out of one sleeve of her housecoat. A tasty titty pops into view and she cocks her head to one side. I darn nearly head my cock to her side, but manage to restrain myself. With difficulty.

"How's that?"

"Very good, but a little more posed, if you know what I mean. Try and flex your – yes! That's it. Smashing."

"Shall I do another one?"

"Please."

This time both bristols gallop out into the open and a spontaneous burst of applause would not be out of order. This girl has certainly got what it takes and I can't wait to take it. She arches backwards and her robe flops on to the floor. There is not much else flopping, I can tell you.

"How's this?" she gasps.

"Unbelievable. Now, careful. Don't break anything. Let me – that's it. Now, a bit more. Fantastic! Back a bit more. Hey, wait a minute. I know what. Get on the bed. Yes. Good. Oh, that's great!"

"Yes it is," she squeaks. "But should you be doing it?"

"Tones up the flesh a treat," I mumble idiotically from the gorge between her breasts. "My goodness me, but you're gollumptuous. I can't see what 'Bedtime Wankie' were on about."

"Bedside Winkie", she corrects me. "Oh. Do you really think I've got a chance?"

"Chance?" I tell her, kicking my jeans over my heels. "I think you're a blooming certainty."

CHAPTER TWO

When I leave Mrs. Sinden's, a large weight is off my mind and the rest of me is feeling much lighter, as well. What a performer that lady is! I feel as if I have been through a suction cleaner a couple of times. Talk about being taken out of yourself. I have to skate round the rest of the lodgings to pick up all the laundry before lunch and the strain of my morning obviously shows.

"Ooh, you're looking completely drained," says Petal resting his hand on my forearm. "Are you all right?"

"Don't do that," I tell him. "How many times do I have to tell you? I'm allergic to being touched."

"Ooh, you are sensitive. I can see you had a bad morning. I had a lovely time in the library. They're ever so nice there. One of the boys, well he's called Jeremy and he's my favourite. He said that his whole life-style had been changed since he worked there. His basics have been broadened out of all recognition."

This comes as no surprise to me and I only hope he will be able to cope with Mr. Warren. Maybe they will be able to strike up a deep and meaningful relationship that will relieve the pressure on my toecap.

Before I can comment further on the subject I hear the crunch of motor car against gravel and look out of the window to see a Rolls pulling up outside the front door. To my amazement, four groovy chicks pile out of it, all fun furs and thigh-length boots, giggling and looking up at the windows.

"Who the hell are they?" I say to myself as much as to anyone else.

"They're wives, ain't they?" says the inmate Legend addressed as Grass, matter-of-factly.

"Wives! ?"

"Yeah. Every Wednesday your wife can visit you for the afternoon."

"Ooh, there's no getting away from them," says Fran distastefully.

"Supposing you don't have a wife, then?" I ask.

"Well, you've had it, haven't you? Old shit-face is dead against immorality."

"But I've got feelings. Just the same as any married bloke."

"If you had 'em strong enough, you'd get married. That's what the Governor thinks, anyhow."

I return my eyes to the crumpet, thinking how unfair it all is. At least, it is good to know that there is some advantage in being married – if you ever got stuck in the nick. Looking at those birds it is difficult to believe that they are spliced. They seem so blooming cheerful compared to most of the wives I know. Maybe this is another result of their old men being in the chokey. Absence makes the heart grow fonder and all that sort of rubbish. They are certainly receiving a lot of attention from the windows and when they disappear inside it is to a sound like someone testing a leaking set of bagpipes. I have hardly got used to their absence when a charabanc arrives, and then another. They are all jam-packed with real sporty looking birds and I feel like I must be one of the few unmarried blokes in the prison. Me, and Fran, of course.

"Ooh, they're like ravening beasts, aren't they?" says Fran. "I think it's disgusting, myself. Like Honeymoon Holiday Camps. All of them arriving down here for only one thing. I'd have too much pride myself. It must take all the romance out of it."

"Yeah," I say, thinking how blooming lucky it is that I had my little session with Mrs. Sinden in the a.m. Without that I could be contemplating knotting myself. You may think it strange that I am wandering about casing the frippet but this is what the place is like. Nobody has asked me to pick any oakum yet – which is just as well as

I wouldn't know which shade to choose – and the only time they lock the door of your cell – oops! sorry – room, is when you are bloody grateful because it is time to start worrying about Fran Warren. At this rate, boredom is going to be my chief enemy unless I can pick up Mrs. Sinden's washing article by article.

I am contemplating this course of action as a serious possibility when another coach-load of bird-life rolls up. I don't know how many blokes there are in the nick but at this rate a lot of them must be moslems. I look down and allow my mince pies to fondle the curvy limbs as the bints trip down the steps of the bus. Blimey! There is a face from the past I recognise. Daisy Deacon. One of sister Rosie's friends from my old Scragg Lane days. She was a raver, was Daisy. I remember her well. Rosie was no angel but Daisy left her standing. I can recall Dad having to lock the door of the potting shed because she was always in there breaking his flower pots. Not intentionally, mind. They just got in the way when she had about three fellahs with her. I might have guessed she'd end up marrying a villain. I wonder – Blimey! Mark II!! There *is* Rosie large as life and twice as tastelessly dressed. What is she doing here? I did not know it was an ordinary visiting day as well. I wonder how she found out where I was? Good old Rosie. I always knew she had a soft spot for me. She does not say too much, but when the chips are down she's in there – one way or another. Not like dad. Dad's attitude really got up my bracket to eyebrow height. Dropping me in the S-H-you-know-what like that.

I abandon thoughts of my evil old man and head for the front entrance where scenes of touching reconciliation are being enacted. Not so much touching as downright groping in some cases.

"Oh, my little lovie-dovie, you're looking marvellous," says one lecherous old sod folding himself round a chick who looks about half his age.

"Hang on a moment," she says coldly. "Are you ninety-nine?"

What a funny question, I think to myself. Surely she knows that by now. What does it matter as long as he's still got some lead in his pencil. He can't have been love's young dream when she first met him.

"I'm sixty-six," he says.

"Well, I'm ninety-nine," she says. "You've got the wrong girl."

The poor bloke looks flabbergasted as well he might. What is she on about? And then I see it! The bird is showing him a lottery ticket which he has read upside down. Could it be that there is hanky panky afoot? My shrewd nature tells me that the answer to that question is a wacking great YES! In that case is it possible that my sister Rosie could be offering herself for the gratification of the lewd and base instincts of the inmates – in some cases, no doubt, almost equal to her own? Again, previous experience suggests a fat "yes" to be the answer to that question. What a carry on! Meanwhile, back at the old homestead, Sidney is probably packing his bucket and spade ready for the Sardinian adventure and imagining the first Cuba Libre of the holiday. The base ingratitude of it all brings tears to your eyes, doesn't it? Not to mine, it doesn't! After what Sidney has lumbered me with I would be prepared to hum "In a Monastery Garden" while Rosie walked naked through an Italian prisoner of war camp. If she wants to come to a sticky end by charabanc – good luck to her. What I want to know is: where's mine?

I am about to address this question to Arthur Legend who is disappearing down the corridor with two birds, when Brownjob suddenly appears beside me and tugs at my sleeve.

"Have you ever thought about it?" he says.

I feel like telling him he must be joking but you have to humour the poor old sod, don't you?

"You mean, dirty thoughts and all that?" I ask him.

Brownjob closes his eyes and winces. "I meant the sacred state of marriage. I know only too well that your thoughts have erred in the other respect. When you see those fortunate men united with the ones they love does it not make you think there is a piece missing from your life?"

I can only nod my head in agreement. "Yes sir," I say humbly.

"I took special care to examine your record, Lea, and I found, just as I expected, that you had never rested your finger on the nuptial knot."

That's all you know, you stupid old berk, I think to myself. There is not a part of the female body I have not had a go at in my time. Since I got those books out of Battersea Public Library I have become an artist at finding parts of the body birds never knew they had. I would have done even better if some thieving bugger had not torn all the diagrams out of the back.

"Lea," continues Brownjob seriously. "Lea, I think that your descent into depravity may have been caused by the lack of a steadying home influence. Faced with the joys and responsibility of a wife and family you could be a new man. Imagine the satisfaction of returning home after a day's honest toil to find your loved one warming your slippers in front of a roaring fire."

"We live in a smokeless zone."

Brownjob shakes his head sadly. "Lea. That response is so typical of your predicament. You are so inhibited, self-orientated and retarded that you cannot be outward going in your feelings for other people. You protect yourself from involvement behind a stockade of insignificant minutia."

"You're probably right, sir," I say. I mean, it is difficult to disagree when you can't understand a word the bloke is saying, isn't it? What disturbs me most about his words is that the stupid old basket realises I am not married. It is therefore going to be difficult for me to get issued with a "wife". Why can't he mind his own bleeding business? Does every bloke inside for making pornographic films have to put up with this invasion of his privacy? I would write to my M.P. about it if I did not know that he was on a fact-finding trip to the Bahamas: studying how Nassau handles its traffic problem or something like that. They don't spare themselves, these blokes, you know. "I'm only saying this for your own good, Lea," burbles Brownjob. "And because I'm a trifle worried about your relationship with Warren."

"Now, wait a minute –" I yelp.

"I know, I know. It's nothing to be ashamed of. I know that the early days in – in an establishment like this can be lonely ones."

"You don't think I'm a –"

"It's not at all unusual if that is any comfort to you, and could, I think, explain your decision to make films which insult and degrade womankind."

The worst thing about all this is that I am beginning to think he may have a point. Perhaps I do hate women. Maybe I am not making love to them, but attacking them. And I did give Fran – I mean, Warren – half my Milky Bar yesterday. Oh, my gawd! "Settle down with a wife and children. That's my advice to you. Bring some stability into your life."

"Yes sir. But it's a bit difficult at the moment."

"I know, Lea, I know." Brownjob gives me a fatherly pat on the shoulder.

"All you can do at the moment is derive what comfort you can from observing the love of others."

A cell door we are passing closes quickly but not before I get a glimpse of what he means. Blimey! They don't waste any time, some of them.

"Think about my words, Lea," says Brownjob, stopping to dismiss me. "If you want psychiatric help it can be arranged."

"On the National Health?"

"On the National Health, Lea."

Sounds too good to miss, doesn't it? If it's free I'm all for it. Dad has got three pairs of false gnashers, two hearing aids and six pairs of specs back at Scraggs Lane. He reckons the Tories are going to take them back and believes in having a few spares up his sleeve.

Brownjob pads off and I go back to my room and try not to feel sorry for myself. Again, thank God I had my little session with Mrs. Sinden, otherwise I might start chewing one of the chair legs. I have just settled down with a stirring epic entitled "Soccer Thug" by one Frank Clegg, when there is a sharp rat-tat-tat on my door. Never one to misinterpret the significance of such things I bid the knocker enter expecting to see Warren's two-tone bonce sidling round the corner primed for another chat on togetherness. In the light of my address from the Governor, I am ready to tell him to push off and start peeling his nuts with a spoke shave but it is not Warren. It is Arthur Ian Legend, Penhurst's other governor.

"How's it going, then?" he says. "Enjoying your book, are you?"

"It's very good," I say. "It's a searing indictment of the sex and violence world of the teenage tearaways. Fearless and outspoken."

"How do you fancy a bit of the other, then?"

Well, I have a lot of respect for Mr. Clegg and his book but nooky does have a greater short-term appeal.

"Very much," I say. "I mean, with birds that is."

I feel it worth making that clear because there are a lot of funny people about.

"Of course, with birds, you berk," says Legend contemptuously. "You don't think I want to travel round your Circle Line, do you? Do I look like a pouf?"

The answer, most assuredly, is no and I try and bring this home to Arthur.

"You must have seen all that totty rolling up," he says. "Some of it is genuine, most of it isn't. Wives and sweethearts. Friends of friends. You know. That kind of thing."

I give him my man of the world nod.

"You'd be amazed how many birds like coming here. They're not getting enough outside and they reckon the thought of a gaol full of sex-starved men rearing to get at them. They feel they're performing a public duty, too. They can justify everything if they can believe that they're saving some poor bastard from going round the twist. They've got what every bird wants, an excuse for doing just as she bleeding well likes."

"So somebody wants to help me, do they?" I say hopefully.

"Any number, son. I've got a right little raver scratching the door of my room at the moment."

"Inside or outside – ?"

"Outside, of course. Don't be funny, son. I'm doing you a favour. I'll leave you alone with your friend if you'd rather."

"No, no," I say hurriedly. "She sounds fantastic, this bird. Great! Lead her to me."

"Are you sure you're up to it?"

"*Up to it?* I'll be out the other side. Don't you worry about me. Give me a couple of minutes, that's all."

I see Arthur on his way and wonder how best to present myself for the love match. Half a bottle of Aqua Velva down the front of my Y-fronts is a foregone conclusion but I reckon this occasion needs more than that. There is not room to swing a cat, so why not return to my bed and await developments? I have always fancied the drowsy, somebody-climbing-in-beside-you bit and here is a first class opportunity to give it a whirl. I shed my threads like they are white hot and kick them under the bed – one does not want to appear untidy, does one? Pausing only to marvel at my mouth-watering loveliness, I slide between the cold sheets and wonder whether you could actually rub down a piece of wood with them. They must make a sandpaper that is several grades finer.

I am looking forward to my encounter with Arthur's friend for a number of reasons, not least being the opportunity it will give me to silence the knockers – I mean the tits with two legs as opposed to the other kind – who have been casting nasturtiums at my relationship with

Fran. When this lady has staggered away to find a full fire bucket my reputation will be restored to its normal Everest proportions.

I turn my head away from the door and burrow into the sheets. I wonder what she will be like. One of the little ravers I saw tripping down the corridor with Legend looked decidedly my cup of Rosie. Wait a minute! The very mention of the name sends cold shivers down my spine. Rosie has no relations in the nick that I know of.

Is it not possible that even now she is padding swiftly towards my cell to do good works? My own sister! How disgusting. With my luck, I cannot afford to lie waiting for the door knob to turn. I leap to my feet and rummage under the bed for my pants. With a bit of luck I may be able to catch up with Legend before he sets the wheels in motion. I race down the corridor and collide with the great man as I dash round the first corner. He has been delayed in a conversation with one of the screws – "and make sure there is plenty of ice. I hate bleeding lukewarm champagne. Yes what is it?"

"I've decided I don't fancy it after all," I blurt out.

"Yerwhat!?"

"I've got this pain. It comes suddenly. I never know when it's going to strike."

"Psschaw!" These letters try to capture the flavour of Legend's mouthwash as it stings my cheek.

"No, straight up –"

"'Straight up'? You couldn't get up with a step ladder. You're bent, mate. I was giving you the benefit of the doubt but you've made it very clear to me now."

"But –"

"No 'buts'. Hopit, before I give you the pleasure of my boot up your backside."

I feel like blurting out the real reason for declining Arthur's favour but deep down inside – so deep that many people never notice it – is a grain of family loyalty that occasionally comes between me and the fulfilment of my ambitions. I do not want to have to admit to Arthur, or anyone else, that Rosie is a ratbag with a one-track mind – and that a dirt track.

I slink back to my room and try to come to grips with Frank Clegg and his powerful novel, but it is no good. I cannot concentrate. I give it a few tries and then go back to bed again. Maybe I will be able to sleep. I usually can whenever I try to read anything. But this time I cannot. I lie in bed and watch the square of blue sky and wonder how I am going to stand living in this place for twelve months with everyone thinking I am bent. Maybe I will be bent by the time I get out. "Knock! Knock!" This time it must be Warren; no doubt offering me a nibble of his Milky Bar. Well, he is not dribbling little pieces of chocolate all over the floor of my cell – I mean room – Oh, dear me, no! I'll soon put a stop to his nonsense. I sit up in bed expectantly but it is not Warren. This is another thing I dislike about the bloke. He is so unreliable.

It is Daisy Deacon with a mouth you could post an ironing board in, tastefully picked out in dayglo paint that threatens to escape up her jumbo-size hooter. This feature trembles as if menaced by the potential avalanche of eye make-up poised above it. Nevertheless, despite a certain lack of subtlety, Daisy is still a sight for sore thighs.

"Well, if it isn't little Timmy Lea," she says breezily. "Do you remember me, love? I used to be a friend of your sister's. I'm sorry to find you in here. Importuning males isn't it?"

This is too much.

"What do you mean!?" I yelp. "I'm as straight as the next man."

"I hope not, dear," she says. "I've just seen him. His blond hair was falling out by its black roots and he walked as if he had just sat on a birthday cake and stolen all the candles."

"Not him! Not him!" I whine. "Listen, Daisy, I'll level with you –"

"Ooh. Sure you're capable?"

"Don't take the piss, Daisy. I'm not really bent. It's just an unfortunate set of circumstances that have got me misunderstood."

"Your mum, wasn't it? I always thought she was inclined to smother you. Know what I mean?"

"No. It was dad who tried to smother me. But it was an accident really. He didn't know mum had put me in the laundry basket. Anyway, Daisy. That's got nothing to do with what I'm on about. I only turned down Arthur's offer because I was scared of bumping into Rosie. I saw her out of the window, you see."

"But she's only visiting."

"Well –"

"Now come on. I know some of the girls are on the game but you don't think your own sister – Timmy, I'm ashamed of you."

"Yes – well – er she can act a bit funny sometimes and I just thought that – well, you know. I'd rather not –"

Daisy quivers with righteous indignation and a ripple goes through her knockers that would show up on a seismograph. "Your sister has been a good friend to Walt and me ever since we both got married," she bridles. "Isn't it natural that she should visit him in his hour of need?"

"Of course, of course," I bleat. "I want to believe you, Daisy." I really do, too. I would much rather accept her explanation even though I don't believe it, than face up to the unpleasant truth. I am like that about lots of things.

"Who are you to point the finger, anyway?"

"Who indeed, Daisy?"

I gaze up at her and turn on my bruised, innocent look. I reckon that this could appeal to the huntress in her and I am not disappointed.

"Talking about my friend like that," she says, looking at the shape of my body underneath the bedclothes. "And your own sister, too."

"Yes." My voice dies away to a whisper and I turn my

head towards the wall. Is it my imagination or is a large tear beginning to form in one of my eyes? It is my imagination. There is a moment's pause and then I feel the reassuring weight of Daisy descending on to the bed. Her hand reaches out and touches my shoulder. I flinch as if I am surprised to feel it.

"You were always a shy boy, weren't you Timmy?"

I feel like saying that compared to Daisy a rape specialist would be a blooming shrinking violet but I keep my mouth shut. When Daisy was knocking around – and I use the expression advisedly – with my sister Rosie, I was a little less experienced than I am now. In fact, I had not broken my duck. It was not until brother-in-law Sidney came upon the scene and introduced me to the window-cleaning business that I began to blossom out.

"You're quite good-looking," continues Daisy stroking my temple with fingers that feel as they have been used for stirring pre-cast concrete. "Pretty hair for a man. I wish my hair curled like that."

"Stick around, kid," I think to myself. "I may be able to save you the price of a home perm kit." I turn over on to my back and gaze up into her generous features hoping that the rest of her is also in a giving frame of mind.

"Poor little Timmy," she says softly. "You never knew what it was for, did you?"

I could give her an argument on that but once I have decided on my plan I must see it through to the bitter end.

"I want," I murmur passionately, "I want –"

This indication of volcano-like emotion struggling to find expression can work wonders with birds and I am not surprised when Daisy's friendly pinkies start creeping under the bedclothes. I try to hold the expression of helpless innocence on my face but it is difficult because I know what Daisy is going to find.

"Oh," she says.

"I don't know what's happened to me," I gasp. "I seem different somehow. Do you think I'm all right?"

"Very definitely," says Daisy climbing swiftly to her feet. "Look the other way – I've got a little surprise for you."

It always puzzles me this: how some of the biggest scrubbers in the world don't fancy you seeing them in the altogether. Once they get to close quarters, anything goes, but they won't let you grab an eyeful of what any kid wandering around an art gallery would get for nothing.

Daisy has not got a beautiful body but there is a lot of it. You have to take the good with the bad. And it is presented with all the subtlety that those lingerie shops in Shaftesbury Avenue can muster. Her bra looks like one of those things your mum used to put round the Christmas cake when you were a kid. And her panties – well, it is not every girl that has "Chase me charlie, I'm the last bus home" embroidered across her nicks in gold thread. Her suspender belt is a very welcome trip down memory lane as far as I am concerned and has little black roses where it makes contact with the stocking tops. I may not know much about art but I know what I like and Mrs. Deacon is bang on target.

"You're looking," she says reproachfully as she leans forward and unhooks her bra. When she does that, I duck instinctively.

"You're beautiful," I say as if a blindfold has just been removed from my eyes. Remember those words: "You're beautiful." I know I labour the point but if you never said anything else to a bird you would get more than your fair share of nooky. That is, basically, what any piece of frippet wants to hear when you open your cakehole. And it has opened more doors than a Metropolitan Police Vehicle Removal Officer – with infinitely more satisfying results, too.

"Do you think so?" she says. That is the kind of stupid thing birds usually say at moments of melting tenderness and though I feel like saying "no, I only said it because I wanted to get my end away" I control myself and continue to gaze into her mush like a moody moggy. She is

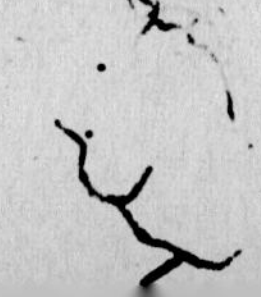

now climbing out of her panties and revealing a pair of thighs like the entrance to a waste disposal unit. Looking at her and remembering her reputation I am not certain if I dare trust my delicate equipment to her tender mercies – I say tender because she is built a bit like one.

I recall that when the American sixth fleet came to town she and Rosie welcomed them so enthusiastically that half the complement of an aircraft carrier had to be helped on to the train back to Portsmouth. The U.S. Navy had to ring up the Russians and ask them to postpone the next Middle East Crisis for a couple of weeks while they recovered. Faced with that kind of animal enthusiasm, am I going to be able to cope?

Now without a stitch, apart from anything left behind in her appendix scar, Daisy pulls back the sheets and slips in beside me.

"Oh," I gulp. "Oh, oh."

I try to sound like a chocolate tester being subjected to a new taste sensation. My barely restrained enthusiasm obviously communicates itself to Daisy because she slumps across my chest so that I can feel her breasts like two heavy bags being dumped on a customs officer's desk.

"Have you ever done this before?" she says. "With a girl?"

I am not certain I like the last bit very much. Have you noticed how difficult it is to try and change people's minds once they have formed an impression of you?

"I've tried," I say bravely.

Her hand is toying with my action man kit again and there is no doubt that Percy is eager for action.

"You shouldn't have any problems," she says encouragingly. "Why don't you put it in?"

"Put it in?" I croak.

"Gordon Bennet! ! Give it here." With an impressive display of champion skills Daisy Deacon puts a hammerlock on my hampton and manoeuvres it into the position where it can do the most damage. "Now push. There we are. That's nice, isn't it? It's nice for me anyway." Just

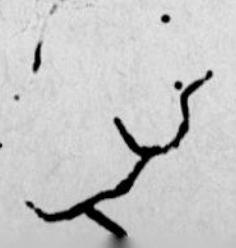

in case I should try and make a bolt for it, Big D grabs hold of the cheeks of my ask-me-no-questions and applies sufficient pressure to make me think she may be attempting a crotch swallow. This is a tempting proposition but the time has now come for me to shed the Robin side of my nature and make with a bit of Batman. From Cock Robbing to Batterman, in fact. With one bound – or extensive wriggle – I am free and directing my energies to a sustained bout of pelvis pounding.

"Oh!" squeaks Daisy. "Oh! Oh! Oh!"

It is as well that my morning exertions with Mrs. Sinden have taken the edge off my appetite as it would be very easy to come to the boil too soon with Daisy. She has the happy knack of giving you the happy knackers and should wear a flashing sign saying "loves it" across her wide Miss Houri bosom.

"You're a quick learner," she gasps. "I'll say that for you."

"There's nothing to it, really, is there?" I pant. "I must have had some kind of blockage in the past."

"You want to stick to girls, dear. It's much better for you in the long run. Much better for them, too. Ooh, that is nice. I feel as if I've just had a champagne enema."

"You don't look as if you have an enema in the world," I say wittily. "Oh, I'm so glad you looked in."

"So am I." And so saying the good lady hauls me to her and proceeds to try and batter a hole in the mattress. Two can play at that game and in less time than it takes to explain to an Irishman that he can move a wheelbarrow from one place to the other without using another wheelbarrow, we are thundering into what I hope is a grandstand finish. Our happy howls are almost too large for the cell and when we at last collapse into a panting heap there falls a silence in which I can sense the rest of the prison holding its collective breath and wondering what is going to happen next.

What happens next is that the door opens and Rosie comes in. There is a pink flush in her cheeks and her eyes appear to be watering but I do not pay too much attention to that.

"Oh!" she says when she sees that her mate is on the job and "O-o-o-h!!!" when she sees who with.

"Hello Rosie," I say. "Been dispensing gruel, have you?"

"Don't be filthy," says Rosie, who is quick to take offence and stupid to boot. "I didn't know you were here." She says it like I organised the whole thing to embarrass her.

"You can't be more surprised to see me than I am to see you. Does Sidney know you're here?"

Rosie's blush deepens. "I don't ask him everything he does. I can see my old friends, can't I?"

"Just what I told him, Rosie dear," says Daisy reaching out for her bra. "I mean, you and my Walt are like brother and sister, aren't you?" She turns to me and squeezes my thigh. "With Walt it's difficult to be anything else. That's why I fell for you. I'm not made of stone, you know. A woman has feelings."

"He's been inside too long, has he?" I ask sympathetically. For some reason my sister finds this funny. She can be very heartless on occasions.

"Something like that," nods Daisy. "Still, I suppose it's the same for all of us, isn't it?"

She swings her legs off the bed and I suddenly wonder what I saw in her – very little from where I was lying as I recall.

"Come on, Rosie," says Daisy. "I want to change Walt's books before the library closes. Don't hang about."

"Look who's talking," sniffs Rosie. "I'd have been away long ago if I hadn't been waiting for you."

They go on rabbiting to each other and by the time Daisy has dressed they have both forgotten I exist.

"When are you off to Sardinia?" I ask Rosie.

"Tomorrow."

"All right for some. Send us a sardine."

"Very funny. I'll see if I can run to a postcard."

"Don't strain yourself."
"Don't tempt me. Ta, ta."
"That was lovely, dear," says Daisy lowering her voice as Rosie goes out of the door. "Remember what I said. Get yourself a girl friend. This phase will soon wear off."
"I'll try," I say.
I close the door and wedge a chair under the handle. The only trouble with this nick is that there are no locks on the inside of the cells, and I need some rest.

CHAPTER THREE

"You never heard of Rita Raver?" says Arthur. "She's a very talented artiste. Her accomplishments cover a multitude of fields. Also, she has a lovely pair of bristols. Stop laughing like that. It's disgusting." He is talking to Grass who is making a noise like a leaking tap in a treacle factory.

"You mean she's coming here to entertain us?"

"Yeah. That's it. You hit it right on the nail. She likes entertaining convicts, doesn't she, Grass? Stop laughing like that! I won't tell you again!"

"She has a very w-wide r-repertoire," stutters Grass practically falling on the floor.

"So would you if you got up to some of the tricks she tries."

"She's a contortionist, is she?" I ask.

"In a manner of speaking," agrees Arthur. "You could put it like that. Or, there again, you could put it like that, or like that, or any blooming way it pleased you."

"She's K.F.C." confides Grass.

"Kilburn Football Club?" I ask.

"Kinky for Convicts! She can't wait to get some shaven headed herbert pressing her backside against the bars."

"Ooh. You make it sound so brutal," squeals Warren whose relationship with Jeremy in the library does not, unfortunately, seem to be an exclusive one. "Brutal, yes, but I must confess, at the same time, *rather* attractive."

"Belt up, poofta," snaps Arthur. "Rita wouldn't ask you to powder her pussy. She wants men, mate, men."

"Don't we all, ducky," shrieks the Chief Fairy. "She's not unique, you know."

"You will be in a minute, if you don't belt up," snarls Arthur. "Blimey, you're more camp than an Indian reservation. Why don't you push off and shrink your jeans."

"I can't shrink them any more. They're skin tight as it is."

"Well, shrink your skin, then. Don't give up so easily."

The man his mother was grooming for the lead in "Gay's the Word" eventually minces off telling anybody who cares to listen that there is no need to be rude, and I ask Arthur a few more questions about the impending visit of Miss Raver.

It appears that Brownjob is very keen on culture for the inmates and likes to import "live" talent as part of his rehabilitation, mingle-with-the-world-outside programme. This does not necessarily have to be of Carnegie Hall standard but capable of performing some artistic endeavour requiring more than a comb and paper for its execution. It also helps if the artist contributes his services for nothing. In fact, when you look at the cast list for the Penhurst Musical Evening this must be the only stipulation. Rita Raver apparently sings and is supported by a cast whose members sound as if they are supported by National Assistance. Len and Alfred Grimble on two pianos, Sandy Sergeant with his singing saw and cellist Alec Smart.

I can control my enthusiasm with ease but am told that all prisoners – sorry, guests – must attend. It is the only compulsory event that I can remember since I arrived at the nick. Apparently in the summer they let you leave the doors open when the nights are warm.

"I've got a nice little number for you," says Arthur with a twinkle in his eye. "Help your rehabilitation a treat, it will. You can look after Rita. Attend to her little whims and needs. You'll find her very grateful. Much better for you than recataloguing your pressed flower collection with that queery."

I am of no mood to argue with him but Fran Warren is furious. "I don't want to appear petulant, pet," he minces. "But really! I have trod the boards, you know, and I would have thought they might have been able to press me into service. What do I have to do to be recognised around here?"

I would have thought that chalking "Love Inn" on the door of your cell – oops! room – and wearing a coloured head band to keep your two-tone hair out of your eyes might have been enough. But you can never tell these days, can you?

"Don't let it get you down," I comfort him. "I'm certain it is going to be the non-event of the year. You're better off out of it."

"I'm sorry, luv," sulks Fran, flapping his hand like a tiny towel. "But I'm taking this very much to heart. I'm really aggravated. I've a good mind to go and do potty all over Legend's spinach."

I counsel him against this because Arthur Ian is definitely the other kind of potty about his spinach. It is amazing how some people get hooked on gardening, isn't it? Often the most unlikely ones, too. Still, I suppose money must have something to do with it. Apparently, according to Arthur, spinach prices are reaching an all time high and with Britain in the Common Market the sky is the limit. Nice to know one is doing one's bit to help the old country even when one is in the nick.

I do not think any more about Fran's outburst and on the night of the concert, report to Brownjob's office where I am supposed to meet Miss Raver. She is not there but Sandy Sergeant is, easily recognisable by the dirty great saw-shaped instrument case he holds between his legs while he sips his sherry.

"No sign of the good lady," beams the Governor. "I expect she has been held up on the road. Not literally, I hope."

We all laugh like drains at the in-joke and Brownjob offers me a glass of sherry. I have never tried the stuff before and am not vastly impressed. For a little shot it does not pack much of a punch and I would rather have a brown ale any day. Mr. Sergeant works for the water board and to listen to him talk about it you would think

the stuff must have soaked clean through him. He has about as much snap, crackle and pop as a damp dish cloth.

"Do you think playing the saw makes you a cut above other musicians?" asks Brownjob who obviously reckons this is his evening for the funnies.

"No, it was my father who put me on to it," says Sergeant seriously.

"Are there any pieces that have been specially written for the saw?" says Brownjob who does not give up easily.

"I saw you last night and got that old feeling," I suggest. Sergeant's face sets into an expression of even deeper gloom.

"I don't think so," he says.

Fortunately Len and Arthur Grimble arrive at that point so there is lots more to talk about. It turns out that they are semi-professionals and they have dinner jackets to prove it. I don't know where they got them from but they look as if they were made with mildewed moss that a couple of snails had conducted a passionate love affair on. I have not seen anything so decrepit since my Uncle Jim rolled up at Rosie's wedding. And when I say rolled, I mean rolled. He looked like the fluff bar on a vacuum cleaner.

"Penge was packed tonight," says Len, chattily – or maybe it was Arthur. Their own wives would have a job telling them apart if they ever bothered to look.

"It's always the same on a Thursday," says Arthur or Len. "It's the late night closing that brings them out."

"And the bingo."

"And the bingo."

They smile at me and I smile back.

"Are you a trustee?" says Len or Arthur.

Before I can answer, Brownjob waves away the suggestion. "Everybody is trusty, here," he beams. "We're the biggest family in South London."

When he says that I feel a lump coming into my throat – or maybe it is a wave of nausea, I don't bother to look.

In the world we live in, ultra innocence seems almost as disgusting as downright villainy.

Next to arrive is a cello – at least, that is what it looks like when the door opens. In fact the cello has a friend who goes everywhere with it. He is the one who manoeuvres it through the door and presumably plays it. He is small and dark and has a nose that looks as if it is trying to look up itself.

"My life, what a day I have had," he pants, patting his glistening forehead with a handkerchief that looks as if it has been used to clean up after a ferret's love-in. "Concert, schmoncert. I feel more like a cup of jasmin tea and a bagel."

"You've had a hard day, Alec?" says Brownjob diplomatically.

"Every day is hard," says Smart. "That you expect when you have your own business. But until today I did not know I was living in a jungle. These people are trying to murder me. I say, all right, so you're my brother-in-law, so why don't you give me a good deal? Isn't blood supposed to be thicker than water? You know what he said?"

"What did he say?" I lose no time in proving what a wonderful half of a double act I could be.

"He said 'so's glue and it's easier to get away from than you are.' That's nice, isn't it? From your own brother-in-law. I don't know what my sister was thinking of when she married him. It wasn't the only offer she had, you know. No! Beautiful girl, she was. They used to call her the Rose of Sidcup. But, she has to throw herself away on him. It's ridiculous. I can still hear my mother crying. I don't think she's stopped since Rachel broke it to her."

"It's not easy, is it?" says Len or Arthur.

"Not easy," echoes Arthur or Len.

"It's difficult," says Sandy Sergeant brightly as if he has just sorted out a taxing clue in a crossword.

I cannot see this lot ever winning an audition for a new T.V. chat show and it is a relief beyond measure when the door bursts open and in sweeps a bird who is nearly as tall as I am. Her hair is piled up on top of her bonce like an imitation busby and she is wearing a long fur coat which flops against her patent leather boots. Her eyes flash and her mouth is a scarlet blur.

"Darlings! I am so desperately sorry," she says punching home each word as if it was a tin tack. "I have had a journey of the utmost hatefulness. If it had been for any other than my favourite engagement I would have abandoned my chariot and waited till all form of road life had forsaken the world before venturing forth again."

During the latter part of her speech she is eyeing me up and down like I am the subject of a "guess your weight" competition and I sense that she likes what she sees.

"My suitcase is without," she continues breathlessly. "I take it I am changing in the usual place?"

I look at Brownjob who nods and waves a hand at me.

"Lea, here, has been favoured as your guide and assistant should you require one. I am certain he will do you proud."

Grammatically this is not quite what I had in mind, but it captures the flavour.

"I'll get your bag," I say. "The curtain's due to go up in a few minutes, isn't it, Sir?"

"I'm certain no one will object to holding it for a few moments," beams Brownjob.

I certainly would not object to holding it for a few moments, or even longer if the occasion arose. Miss Raver is clearly an artistic bird and they are often the best when it comes to a spot of in and out. All that frustrated creativity can emerge from some very funny places.

"I'll be as quick as I can, darlings," breathes Rita. "I'm certain it's going to be a tremendous experience for all of us."

She is right there but I don't know that at the time. I grab her suitcase and she leads the way down the corridor asking me whether I have a theatrical bent. I think she means Warren for a moment before I catch on. The Gents near the main hall has been turned into her dressing room and I come over all middle class standing there with her in front of the corrugated porcelain. Well, it's not nice, is it? I don't go poking my nose into Ladies' Lavs. I don't like to think about things like that.

"Charming," she says as I put her suitcase on a trestle table in front of the mirror. "They might have rubbed that out."

I follow her eyes and I have to agree with her. You do get some funny people about. To prove what a gent I am, I get a bit of bog paper, gob on it and stick it over the offending message so that only "Wellington Boots" remains uncovered.

"Thank you," she says. "That's very sweet of you."

She opens her suitcase and I turn to go. "Do you think you could be an absolute angel and find a heater?" she purrs. "It is rather cold in here."

She is not kidding. Only a penguin could relish a pee in these surroundings.

"I'll have a look," I say. I leg it back to Brownjob who is holding his sherry bottle up to the light and making a mark on it with a pencil. He seems embarrassed to see me. "Someone's been having a crafty swig, have they?" I ask, to put him at his ease.

"Yes," says Brownjob. "I fear there may be a thief about."

"Oh dear. You can't trust anyone these days, can you?" We nod wisely at each other.

"Miss Raver wants an electric chair – I mean fire!" I yelp. I do wish I had not said that because it obviously upsets Brownjob considerably. Him being against capital punishment and all that kind of caper. Eventually I leave him making another mark on his sherry bottle and pad back to Miss Raver with the spoils.

To my surprise she is now wearing a long taffeta dressing-gown and her discarded clothes are lying on the table.

"You've got one," she says. "Good. I've found where you can plug it in. Over here." I do as she suggests and she immediately straddles the fire and makes contented cooing noises.

"Well – er, I'll leave you to it," I say. "Good luck. When will you need me again?"

"Don't go away," she says. "I need you now. You have nothing against sex with a perfect stranger, do you?"

I have nothing against sex with a bloody awful stranger, but I am a bit surprised, to put it mildly. Maybe I have misheard her.

"It's my vocal chords," she continues. "I can't get my range unless I've had sex. It relaxes me."

She opens her dressing-gown to give me an idea of what she is on about. She is very scrawny but after some of the birds I have been getting lately, I am not going to write to my M.P. about it.

"What, now?" I say.

"I'd have thought you might have found the idea a trifle appealing. You can't be exactly inundated with female company."

"Only in a manner of speaking," I say, wondering what she is on about.

"Help me," she murmurs stretching out a hand. "Remember, it's for art."

"Art who?" I croak as her fingers keep going for my growing groin.

"Silly boy," she husks. "You know what I mean."

She takes a step towards me and flinging open her dressing-gown wraps it around both of us.

"Steady on!" I mutter. "The curtain goes up in a minute."

"Emulate it, darling."

"I beg your pardon?!" I mean, there is no need to be like that, is there?

"Enter me."

For a second I think she means in Crufts or something, and then I get her drift. She is playing the front of my trousers like there is a keyboard there and suddenly she launches herself at my cakehole and thrashes my lips with her mouth. Some men might be able to think about thinning out their radishes at a time like this, but I am not one of them. I can no more deny her what she so clearly wants than whistle "God Save the Queen" with a mouthful of cocoa powder. Half pushed, half pulling, I stagger backwards in to an empty cubicle and find Miss Raver attacking the front of my trousers like she is trying to rip up bits of material for bandages. Percy has no sooner tasted freedom than she is ruckling my big end against the cistern and making "Rita wants it" type noises. Her impassioned mumblings are unnecessary because a half-deaf Trappist Monk who had only seen drawings of women on cave walls would have a clear idea of what she had in mind.

"Madam, please," I murmur. "Let's wrestle on the trestle. I was never one to uncoil it in the toilet."

My plea for sanitary must come home to her because she releases her half Nelson on my hampton and allows herself to be led back to the comparative decorum of her dressing table. Hardly an apt description of the article, I think to myself as I press her ninety per cent nude body back to the planks and prepare to muster my cluster.

"Oh, that's heaven," she murmurs as I disappear into her like half a pound of beef dripping on to a hot griddle. "Absolute heaven."

It is not bad for me, either, and the next few moments represent a rare advance on trying to push your old man through an electric fan without hitting the blades. If Rita Raver is half such a good performer in an upright position then her concert should be really something. We are winding up to a crescendo when there is a bang on the door and a voice shouts "Overture and beginners". I nearly jump out of her skin but Rita takes it all very coolly – she gets so much practice, I imagine.

"They're a bit late, aren't they darling?" she murmurs. "I made all the overtures and you're obviously not a beginner."

This sophisticated banter could, no doubt, continue to

the early hours of the morning but Rita indicates that she feels ready for the fray and we drift apart like a couple of pieces of half-chewed toffee being prised off a clog. Talking about "fray", my old man is practically in that condition and I am glad to see that there is no smoke rising from the area covered by my jockey briefs.

"Be an angel and find me a cup of tea," breathes Rita beginning to pat her face into place in the mirror. "I only do a short spot to begin with."

I trot off to the kitchen but everything is locked up. They must have gone to the concert. The sound of rhythmic stamping suggests that someone has. I get to the hall and the mood is about as ugly as Arthur Legend's passport photo.

"Why are we waiting?" chant the audience.

"We want Rita! We want Rita!"

"Gentlemen, please!" implores Brownjob rising to his feet in the front row. "Miss Raver has been detained by traffic but even at this moment is preparing to entertain you. May I suggest that you would be better employed in conserving your energies to give her a real Penhurst welcome, rather than behaving in this unseemly fashion."

"Get 'em orf!" shouts an anonymous voice from the fifth row.

"That kind of remark won't help anyone," snaps Brownjob beginning to lose his cool.

What kind of remark would help, we never know, because Rita sweeps on to the stage and Brownjob sits down swiftly. I have vaguely wondered what Rita will sound like but none of my surmises come anywhere near the reality. Would you believe, a baritone? I never visualised a bird singing "The Road to the Isles" before, but she does a very good job with it. She is wearing a low cut dress just so you can have no difficulty in checking that she has smaller knockers than the doors of a semi-detached doll's house and is wearing a sheath dress that, with her piled up barnet, makes her look like a roll of linoleum with a French loaf wedged on the top of it. I may sound unkind but she does not make the best of herself.

After the "Road to the Isles" we get "The Fishermen of England" and "Captain, art thou sleeping there below?" and I am beginning to wonder what a short spot is. The inmates go wild every time she closes her cakehole and I can see the attraction of playing to prison audiences. These blokes will go crazy for anything if it is wearing a skirt.

I skip back to the gents to wait for her and she sweeps past me like she has just swum the Atlantic towing the Q.E.II.

"You were fantastic," I humour her. "I've never heard anything like it."

"You mean the applause?"

"Er – yes," I nod. "I'm sorry, but the kitchen was closed. I couldn't raise a cup of tea."

"It doesn't matter. We'll do it again."

"You mean – ?"

"Yes, quick. I'm on in another five minutes."

Before I can say "music stand" she has wriggled out of her dress and is pushing her nicks down to floor level.

"Does this really make a difference to your singing?" I ask.

"Of course, darling. You don't want me to dry up, do you?"

"No – but –"

"Come on. I can feel myself going all stiff."

It is funny she should say that because Percy is experiencing exactly the same problem. He has not said no to anything since Evie Crabtree nearly turned his foreskin into a five skin with a bit of clumsy zipping up behind the children's playground on Clapham Common in '67.

By the cringe, but she was game that Evie. She had hung around longer than any partridge and her enthusiasm knew no end – it certainly did not know mine after our little accident. I still get a twinge every time I think of her.

Anyhow, that is all a long cry from the long lady who is now stretched out on the trestle table looking at me expectantly.

"Come on, you beast," she husks. "I know what you're in for. The Governor whispered it to me."

She gives a wriggle of ecstasy and starts groping for my groin. Oh dear, my reputation has obviously got a lot to answer for. If only they knew.

"I'm not really like that," I say plaintively. "It's all got a bit exaggerated."

"That's what they all say, darling." She gives another delicate little wriggle like a chicken settling in to a dust bath and I find my trousers magically disappearing for a reunion with my ankles.

"Come on," she urges. "Ars gratia artis."

They do say some coarse things, these birds, when they get worked up, don't they? Still, I suppose it is my own fault for being so irresistible.

"How many intervals are there?" I ask, as my thighs take up their familiar position against the edge of the table.

When I get back to the auditorium, Sandy Sergeant and his singing saw are in full swing, or maybe I should say swine. The noise sounds like a pig with wind, and is enough to make a tom cat cringe.

"By gawd but I'd like to introduce him to that bugger with the big violin," says one inmate, shaking his head in disgust. "If he had used that thing instead of a bow all our troubles would be over."

So I have missed Alec Smart as well. Miss Raver's private acts must be longer than the ones she does on stage – and with a darn sight more audience appeal, too.

I am trying to concentrate on the finer points of Sergeant's wrist action when I am distracted by a chorus of wolf whistles. Surely my fellow inmates are not so desperate that sallow Sandy Sergeant has suddenly become invested with some mysterious sex appeal? The answer, thankfully, is no. Filing down the gangway are a party of birds. They do not look like contestants for the Miss Universe Contest but this may have something to do with their clobber. Shapeless grey dresses never did a lot for anyone.

"Who the hell are they?" I ask the bloke next to me who has his fingers jammed into his trap up to the knuckles.

"That's our sister prison: St. Belters."

"'Sister prison'"! Blimey! Times haven't half changed since the rest of my family were in the nick. I can see Brownjob's hand in this. If he had his way, we would probably all be sharing cells together. Not a bad idea when you think about it. You could cut accommodation in half without getting any complaints.

"Do they come here often?"

"You must be joking. The Governor is very keen on fraternisation. We reciprocate sometimes."

"As long as it doesn't affect your eyesight."

We turn our attention to the two rows of benches that have been reserved for the girls and I realise why all the biggest, meanest, nastiest geezers have been crowding in on them. Like sultanas being stirred into a Christmas pudding the birds disappear into the audience until you would be pushed to find two sitting next to each other.

"Boy, there's instant romance for you," I say to the bloke next to me, but he has gone. The only thing that does not change its position is the hideous row of Sandy Sergeant's saw which seems to be permanently wedged in my earhole. I may be allergic to this but everybody else appears to have forgotten its existence. When the last wavering note ceases to disturb my tooth fillings there is a silence like that which greets an away goal at Anfield Road. Everybody must obviously have something better to do with their hands. Brownjob makes a brave effort at stirring up some applause from the front row but he is wasting his time. Couples are slipping away out of the hall and those remaining are getting acquainted faster than a couple of sex-starved rabbits hearing the combine harvester approaching.

"Looking after Miss Raver, are you, Lea? She seems to be in very good voice." Brownjob is sweeping past en route to a half-time suck of the lemons. His words make me wonder what is in store for me. Rita Raver is no doubt eager to keep those vocal chords well and truly lubricated whilst I feel more like that cup of tea she was rabbiting on about.

"I'm doing what I can, sir," I say dutifully.

"Good work, Lea. Keep it up. That's all I ask of any of my chaps."

I smile bravely and Brownjob goes on his way. He is a good man and a breath of spring to the penal system as this country knows it. I only wish my own penal system was feeling in better nick at the moment. Maybe I should give the second half a miss and slide off back to my room. With this in mind, I am making tracks past the Gents when the door opens and Miss Raver pops her nut out.

"Just the man I'm looking for," she hisses. "Come here, I need you."

"I've just remembered I need to finish embroidering my mail-bag," I whine. "They're judging tomorrow and I've set my heart on a credit."

"Don't forsake me now, Lea," she breathes. "I'm well in with the Governor and I can get you anything you want. All I ask is a little co-operation. I've got to open the second half in a few minutes and I'm feeling parched."

"I'm not feeling like Lake Windermere, myself," I croak. "Surely you can knock off a few stanzas without all this palava?"

"Please! !" sobs Raver the Craver. "Can't you see that music is my life?"

I reckon I could be excused for getting that one wrong but I do not say anything. In the circumstances there does not seem to be much point.

"Listen," I say firmly. "This is the last time. My baton's

beginning to feel as if it's been sat on. I like music as much as the next man, but there is a limit to what I can do to subsidise the arts."

"You and your long words," says Rita, playfully tweaking my sense of responsibility. "Just help me limber up for the second half and we'll discuss the rest of my performance later."

The thought appeals to me about as much as mating my hampton with a bacon slicer but again I keep a grip on the word power. That part of Miss Raver that I am now beginning to know much better than the back of my hand is once again twinkling before me and Percy, bless him, is rising to the occasion with that blind reckless courage that characterised those poor sods who rode into the Valley of Death. Not a bad name for it, either, I think to myself as Rita's pincer-like thighs lock round my stripling frame. When she gets a grip of me, I know how a blocked-up drain must feel just before that rubber cup thing is bashed up and down over the plughole. If what I am going through is not enough – and it is, believe me – Rita starts singing while I am on the job. This might be all right, but "Old Man River"? Do me a favour! She makes Paul Robeson seem like Petula Clark. The whole thing is more than my nervous system can stand and by the time I limp out of the door I feel as I have passed through both sides of a revolving door at the same time. Nothing, repeat nothing, is going to get me in that room again.

I return to the hall and it is amazing how few people there seem to be about. No sign of a bird of any description. Even Brownjob is beginning to peer about him anxiously as the curtain goes up. Rita gives us the "Road to Mandalay" and "The Vulgar Boatman" and there is no doubt that her vocal chords seem to thrive on a spot of in-and-out. Forget crystal glasses. I reckon she could shatter a piss pot at forty paces.

"Ooh. She's a nasty cow," says Warren petulantly, as he flutters to my side.

"I'm surprised you're listening," I say to him. "I thought you'd gone off in a huff."

Warren smiles evilly. "I'm feeling better now," he says. "You're not looking so good, though. She been putting you through it, has she?"

"Oh, no," I say as a thought strikes me. "She's a wonderful performer. Greasepaint in her veins. One of the old school. I think you'd have a lot in common."

"I'm not going to have much chance to find out," sniffs Fran.

"Yes you are. I've got to telephone about her car. Why don't you pop down and see if she wants anything?"

Rita is coming off the stage to generous and, I think, grateful, applause and Warren looks thoughtful.

"I'm not certain I want to."

"Oh, go on!"

"Oh, all right! I'll just stick my head round the door. One has to say hello to a fellow thespian, doesn't one?"

I don't reckon she is one of those, mate, I think to myself, but no doubt you'll find out soon enough.

I breathe a sigh of relief and settle down to enjoy Len and Arthur Grimble at two pianos. Trotting out on to the stage they look like a couple of penguins with dandruff. They face the audience, hitch up their sleeves, nod to each other and sit down on their stools – which collapse simultaneously. Those remaining in the audience laugh themselves sick and for a moment I wonder if this is supposed to be a comedy act. The impression is virtually confirmed when Len and Arthur struggle to their feet and, gazing at each other with expressions approaching the terrified, bring their mitts down hard on the keyboards causing the pianos to collapse dramatically. There is a splintering noise and one of the concert grands sags through the stage like an ocean liner going down. Immediately the howl from the audience is drowned by a louder squeal from the shattered rostrum.

"Get it off! Get it off!" howls a voice in anguish and suddenly the naked head and shoulders of a man and woman appear through the stage. They are attempting to manoeuvre the stricken piano and are soon joined by several more naked struggling bodies. I am reminded of an illustration of Hell I saw in one of my old schoolbooks. Standing there in their shabby dinner jackets, Len and Arthur Grimble gaze down upon the scene as if unable to believe their eyes.

It occurs to me that two things have happened:

(1) Somebody has sabotaged the pianos and stools
(2) The ladies from St. Belters and half the blokes in the hall have been getting better acquainted beneath the stage.

Before I can discuss these interesting theories with anyone there are fresh developments. Sandy Sergeant rushes to the edge of the stage almost in tears. Somebody has broken his saw! No sooner has this terrible news sunk in to a totally uninterested audience than Fran Warren dashes down the aisle with Rita Raver in hot – and I mean, hot – pursuit. There is an expression of desperate terror in his eyes and the shirt is torn half off his back.

"Help, help, help! Rape!" he screams as Rita closes the distance between them to inches. It is becoming clear to me that things could easily get out of hand – but, luckily, Arthur or Len is equal to the challenge. Dropping on both knees he shuffles to the keyboard of his floor level instrument and begins to play The National Anthem.

CHAPTER FOUR

"Fancy him having a nervous breakdown," says Warren. "He can't have been up to it, can he?"

"I hated it when he cried," says Grass. "I can't bear to see a grown man cry."

"We'll never see his like again, mark my words," says Legend, shaking his head. "That stupid old twit was one in a million."

"I liked him," says Warren.

Legend grabs Warren by the lapels of his reefer jacket. "I liked him too," he says.

"We all liked him. He was the best governor this bleeding nick ever had. And he's gone! All because of you, you miserable little basket!"

"Oh, come on, now," squeals Warren. "It's no good pointing the finger at me. It wasn't my fault you were all carrying on like that. Sufficient unto the day is the evil in him who evil thinks."

"What are you talking about?" snarls Legend. "You sawed the pianos up, didn't you?"

"I was upset," mumbles Warren.

"Upset!" Legend waves his plaster cast under Warren's twitching nostrils. "I was bleeding upset and all, wasn't I? What do you think this is? Icing sugar? You try balancing a grand piano on your hampton and tell me what it feels like! You might have killed someone."

"Ooh, how many times do I have to say I'm sorry? You do go on."

"It's no good exciting yourself, guv," says Grass soothingly. "It's all water that's been passed under the bridge now."

"Yeah. I suppose you're right," agrees Legend grudgingly. "I just wish I could make this little prick realise what he's done, that's all. The next bloke we get is not going to be like Brownjob."

I realise how true his words are when, next day, I am trimming the verges by the front entrance to the prison. I am enjoying the sunshine and picking the next England Soccer team to win the World Cup when a short, sharp blast on a motor horn brings me back to the present. I look up and see a hook-nosed geezer with eyes like mouse droppings on a bowl of lard. He is beckoning to me from the window of a car.

"When did you last polish your shoes?" he says.

"They're suedes," I tell him.

"Suedes what?"

"Suedes what I bought when I was outside."

The grim-faced geezer closes his eyes to razor slits. "Call me Sir when you address me," he hisses. "And don't make me a sounding board for your bucolic sense of humour. I am the new Governor and I can see immediately that there are going to be a number of changes around here." One of the first should feature your underwear, I think to myself, but I don't let on. It does not seem the right moment to start chatting about personal freshness.

"Firm is the name and firmness is my stock in trade," continues grizzle-guts. "Where is the rest of your party and who is in charge of it?"

"There isn't one, and nobody," I say. "Balfour suggested I came down here."

"Balfour?"

"He's president of the gardening committee."

"In future, you will address warders as 'Mr.'" says our new governor icily.

"Oh, he's not one of the guardians – I mean warders. He's a guest."

"A what! ! ?"

"An inmate," I gulp.

"You mean a prisoner! This is a prison. Let us have no illusions about that. You are here because you have offended against society and you merit punishment. I am here to administer that punishment."

He sounds as if he is chipping the words off the side of a glacier with an alpenstock (look it up if you don't know what it means. When you have sat in as many doctors' waiting rooms as I have, you can't help being well read).

Blimey! It is so difficult, isn't it? One moment they tell you one thing, the next, another. If I had known it was going to be like this I would have opted for Holloway right from the start.

"Yes, sir," I say meekly. The new Governor is not alone in the back seat of the Daimler. There is a bird with him. Slim and severe but I would not climb over her to get to Harold Wilson. She is looking at me with an expression of dispassionate interest etched across her features – rather like a medical student examining a cold germ under a microscope. She is wearing a wedding ring and must presumably be Mrs. Firm. Good. Things are looking up. I gaze into her eyes as if I can see the winner of the four-thirty written around her irises but she turns away and stifles a yawn. Charming! Just what I need to feel really magnetic.

"Get in the front!" snaps the Guv'nor. "I'm taking you back."

The way he says it, I feel as if I have been caught trying to saw through the main gates with a hacksaw. I give Mrs. Governor another burning glance that seems to be capable of sending her off to sleep and get in beside the driver who raises his eyes sympathetically.

"My God, but there are going to be some changes here," snarls the great man behind me. "President of the Gardening Committee indeed!"

"Careful, George. Don't get excited," says Mrs. F. very deadpan. "Remember what the doctor said."

The Governor does not answer that one because he is doing a lot of coughing and it is Mrs. F. who is the next to speak. "He might be ideal," she says.

I turn round swiftly and find that they are both looking

at me. The Governor turns away and gazes out of the window.

"Humf!" he says.

I might be ideal for what? What is Mrs. F. mulling over behind those cool, blue eyes? I hope she does not reckon me for some kind of diabolical experiment. There must be a law to protect people against things like that.

I do not get a lot more chance to read the answer from her inscrutable mug because the car stops outside the main building and George leaps out like it is in danger of catching fire. Mrs. F. waits till he is out of earshot and suddenly switches her eyes to me.

"When were you born?" she says, almost eagerly.

"Five. Eleven. Fifty," I tell her.

"And where?"

"Lambeth."

"Oh," she nods, and I can see her lips moving as if she is counting.

"Where were you born?" I say cheerfully.

"Don't be impertinent." She clicks back to normal like a self-correcting milometer registering that your journey is over. I don't reckon that she is going to be remembering what I looked like first thing in the morning at this rate. George goes through the front door like a circular saw and she follows him, with my eyes stuck to her shapely legs like burrs.

"Take me to the Harbour Club," I say to the driver.

"Piss off!"

I get out and apologise to the driver for catching him below the lughole with my hoe. "It was an accident, really it was," I tell him.

I don't think he believes me because he says something very nasty as he drives off nearly taking my sleeve with him – some of those door handles can be very dangerous.

There is no doubt about it, George Firm is a man of his word. That very night, we are locked in our cells and some of the more friendly warders who used to act as mail men with the outside world disappear faster than a tin of vaseline at a Gay Liberation Front Gang Bang. Exercise periods are introduced and our comparative freedom is severely curtailed.

"It's diabolical," snorts Legend. "The place is becoming like a bleeding prison! Strewth, I wish I'd done that bleeding Warren when I first clapped eyes on him."

"It's the spinach that's breaking my heart," moans Grass. "It needs very careful nurturing, that stuff, and I just can't get near it. Firm's cut off the fertiliser, too."

"Bastard!" storms Legend. "After all the work we've put in. Somebody ought to do something about him. Even the meanest sods let you work on the prison farm."

"Shut up and keep humping those rocks!" bawls one of the new warders who is enjoying making our lives a misery. "You want the Governor to have a nice rockery, don't you?"

"I'd like to arrange these stones on his grave so that the werewolves couldn't get at him," pants Legend. "Blimey! I shouldn't get lumbered with this kind of detail at my age. I've got a weak heart, you know. My doctor's going to be in touch about this. If I drop down dead there's going to be trouble."

"Especially if you do it before you've finished moving those stones," says the unlovable screw. "Now, get a move on!"

The surface we are working on is outside the Governor's wing and it is the fourth site he has chosen. You do not have to have a high I.Q. to reckon that Firm is coming a touch of the hard man. As we sweat I look up at the windows and there is Mrs. F. staring down at us with her arms folded. She is wearing a white coat and an expression which I believe is called enigmatic. Once again, I sense myself being singled out for special attention but this may be my excitable imagination. The lady is also wearing rimless specs and she looks very poised and professional. Like those birds in the movies who play the cold, super-efficient secretary until the last reel when the boss takes off the glasses, lets down the hair and says:

"Why, Miss Trimbody, you're beautiful!" just like you knew he was going to do from the first moment she spilt coffee all over his goolies at the new Client presentation – and when you noticed that she was played by Doris Day. I find myself fancying Mrs. Firm rotten but my chances of getting her seem less likely than Fran Warren winning the Mr. Universe title. I think about her manually that night and the next morning I find myself tracing her name on a dirty window pane. Prudence. One of the blokes heard George calling her that. Prudence. It's got class, hasn't it? Ladylike but with a touch of hidden Jenny say quoits as the French put it in their own inimitable fashion. I am still thinking about her when one of the new screws comes up to me in the exercise yard. His face is as mean as a ½p tip and his teeth look like they started life as the tip-up targets on a seaside rifle range.

"Mrs. Firm wants to see you," he says.

"Who, me?"

"You're Lea, aren't you?"

"Yes."

"Well, come on, then. Step lively. The minute she's seen you she can get down to doing something useful."

Charming lot of bastards, aren't they? No wonder many of our more refined criminals choose to live abroad. I pad along after the nauseous nark, wondering what Prudence wants with me. It can't be that, can it? Can it? The minute I see her, I know the answer. No.

She is sitting behind a desk and wearing a white coat that looks as if it only contains slightly more starch than she does. She taps her specs on to the bridge of her nose and addresses me whilst looking out of the window as if speaking into a microphone suspended from the pelmet.

"I have been examining your record here," she says, "and there is no doubt that you are just what I'm looking for." Can't be bad, can it? "Rotten to the core. Not only appearing in pornographic films but helping to produce them as well."

I am past arguing so I follow her eyes out of the window. Legend and friends are moving the rockery again. At least I have been spared that. Oh dear, Grass is having a crafty leak over the petunias. Mrs. Firm and I haul our eyes indoors quickly. "I am a trained psychiatrist and I think I can help you. Have you ever been hypnotised?"

Mrs. F. removes her specs with a sweeping gesture and stares into my mince pies like she is trying to look out of the back of my bonce.

"No," I say. "Well, there was this bloke at the British Legion, but he just wanted to pour a bucket of water down the front of my trousers."

Mrs. F. shudders. "I am quite serious," she says. "I believe that I can reprogramme you under hypnosis. Snitzel and Gobbler have done some wonderful work with the Bangkwiki tribe."

"Really?" I say.

"Yes. Quite remarkable. They have changed the whole style of their cave drawings. From works of a very elemental sexual nature they have switched, under hypnosis, to producing highly civilised microcosms of the contemporary environment."

She holds up what looks like a kid's drawing full of blokes stabbing each other in the back. It could be the office party in an advertising agency, only there is not enough blood around.

"I don't reckon that's a big advance, myself," I say. "I mean, you get enough of that on the telly, don't you?"

Mrs. F. allows a long shudder to run through her body – I only wish she would allow me to keep it company.

"You need help," she says dramatically. "You need help badly. It's probably your inability to face up to the realities of contemporary life that makes you fall back into this perverted world of sexual fantasy."

"You may well be right," I say. "I do get a bit cheesed off with the party political broadcasts sometimes."

Mrs. F. nods briskly as if I have confirmed her worst suspicions.

"I'm going to take you right back to the very bedrock of your spiritual degradation," she says.

"You mean Clapham Common?"

"No. I'm speaking metaphorically."

I wish she would stick to English because I don't understand a word of these new international languages. They will never catch on, anyway. Who wants to learn a language nobody else speaks? You can't go to Esperant for your holidays, can you?

"I'm going to put you in a trance and then I'm going to show you some quite disgusting photographs," she says. "While you look at them I will probe your subconscious."

Well, I will try anything once and it does not sound too bad, does it? I would not have any objections to probing Mrs. Firm should the opportunity become available.

"It's all right, is it?" I say anxiously. "I mean, I can't come to any harm, can I?"

"Nothing worse than what has already befallen you," says Mrs. F. seriously. "All you will feel is a revulsion for pornography when you emerge from hypnosis."

"You've had a lot of experience have you? – I mean of hypnosis, of course."

Mrs. F. looks slightly uncomfortable. "This form of treatment for the psychologically disturbed is in its infancy so nobody has had a great deal of experience. Rest assured though that it is quite harmless."

"What do you mean 'harmless'?" I bleat. "I'll still be able to get it up, won't I? I mean, I might want to get married one day."

Mrs. F. blushes. "Your ability to enjoy a healthy physical relationship with the girl you eventually marry will be in no way impaired. It is only the obscene side of your nature that will be expunged."

"It's a bit difficult to separate the two with me," I say, beginning to get worried. "Don't you reckon you need a more open and shut case to practice on?"

"No," says Mrs. F. firmly. "You are just right. Your

horoscope is also propitious. If the treatment will work with a person of your depraved tendencies, then we stand on the brink of a breakthrough."

She puts it so nicely, doesn't she? "Supposing I say no."

Mrs. F. looks out of the window. "Then agricultural labour beckons."

I suppose she means the poxy rock garden. Legend is now doubled up holding his back and seems to have lost about three stone since the days when he was dishing out glasses of sherry.

"All right," I say. "When do you want to start?"

"Now. Come and sit down facing me."

I notice that she is tapping a pile of postcards against the table. These must be the porn pics she was on about. Surely having a butchers at them is not going to put me off exercising my spam ram?

I sit down and stare into Mrs. Firm's bluey grey eyes. Prudence. What a pretty name. If only she knew what she suffered at my hands last night.

"Close your eyes and open them when I tell you. I want you to empty your mind of all thoughts and impressions, Relax everything. When you open your eyes, concentrate on looking into the very centre of mine."

I close my eyes obediently and try to do as she says, but I keep getting an impression of a bird sitting down naked from the waist up, except for a string of pearls. Her.

"Open your eyes."

I stare intently.

"Close. Open. Close. Now, look at this."

I accept the photograph and – Phew! Not bad. Not bad at all. This bird is lying on a sofa with a copy of "The Motor Cycle" and the bloke is getting stuck into her like she is a four course meal. Pity about the socks, though. They do detract from the glamour.

Mrs. F's hand reaches out. "Close your eyes."

I feel her removing the photograph.

"Open." She is taking a quick glance at the photograph but jerks her eyes back to mine. "Close." Now I can see

Prudence lying on the sofa instead of the bird. And I don't dislike the idea, either.

"Open." I concentrate on gazing into the very centre of Mrs. F's eyes. She blinks and then shakes her head as if clearing it after a blow.

"C-close." Another photograph is pushed into my hand.

"Open. Look at me, then look at the photograph."

I gaze down and – oh dear! That really is rather naughty. Very nice, though. Hey, wait a minute. I'm not supposed to be thinking that.

"You are disgusted?" hisses Mrs. F. It comes out as more of a question than a statement of fact. I take another look at the photograph and shake my head.

"Close!" Mrs. F. sounds desperate. "Concentrate on what they were doing. Feel revulsion! Revulsion! Revulsion! Revulsion!" Suddenly I feel her hand on top of mine and her finger nails digging into my flesh. I open my eyes instantly and give the good lady the famous Lea slow burn guaranteed to steam open Russian-issue buff envelopes.

"Feel," I murmur. "Feel. Feel, feel."

I take her hand gently in mine, turn it over and start to knead her soft palm – experienced readers will realise that I also need her soft something else, but it is no good rushing things. Her eyes feed on mine and it is clear to me that our roles have been reversed. I am hypnotising her. If this is the case, then I have her in my power and who knows what evil tricks I could get up to? Well, I know for a start, so what am I waiting for?

"Look at the photograph," I say firmly. "Look at it."

Without taking her eyes from mine, Mrs. F. reaches across the desk and fumbles for the photo of Miss Guzzle enjoying her pork lolly.

"Look!" I breathe.

Mrs. F's lips tremble like a flutterby's wings and she breaks our glance like it is a stick of barley sugar. She gazes at the photo, gulps, looks again and slowly closes her eyes, tilting her head back towards the ceiling.

"O-o-o-h," she gurgles.

"You like the idea, don't you?" says the evil weevil inside me. Mrs. Firm's eyes close tight shut and she nods slowly. There is a pause and then her eyes open and she nods slowly. Our eyes are now mating. This is O.K. for starters but both of us clearly have sympathy for the needs of the rest of our bodies. Mrs. F. climbs out of her chair and comes round the desk towards me. I hold out my hand and she takes it and draws me towards a button backed settee that looks like a plateful of neatly arranged Ravioli.

"Lie down," she says. "I want to do it to you."

I suppose, somewhere in the Outer Hebrides or the Inner Circle, there is someone who would say "No thanks, I've got to catalogue my beer mat collection" but such a creature has little in Wandsworth Common with me.

Obediently I sink back against the settee and gaze upon the stimulating sight of Mrs. F. dropping to her knees and preparing to administer the kiss of life. With a refinement and delicacy worthy of her name, she takes my zipper between finger and thumb and draws it smoothly down towards the root of many of my problems. Impatient Percy quivers like a python awakening after a winter's kip and as Mrs. F. presses forward to enter the tent flap of my y-fronts, I snatch a diplomatic glance at the outside world. Legend, Grass and a couple of friends are watching open-mouthed through the window. Surprise is not so much written on their features as etched with a pneumatic drill.

Mrs. F. has now uncovered my action man kit and having gazed at it like it is some freshly discovered art treasure she lovingly and longingly – o-o-o-o-o-h! My eyes float up to the ceiling like ping-pong balls imprisoned at the bottom of a swimming bath and I feel as if I have been plugged into a jar of electric worms.

"Oo-a-a-ah!"

The sentiment is familiar but the sound does not leap from my cakehole. I avert my peepers and pass from the happy sight of Mrs. F. in full slurp to that of husband George sliding down the closed door through which he has just entered. His face has turned an unhealthy white colour which, as I watch it, is fast changing to blue.

"A-a-a-gh!!" he croaks and disappears behind the settee.

Outside on the lawn Arthur Ian Legend is giving a thumbs up sign.

CHAPTER FIVE

"Heart attack?" says Grass. "Blimey, that's not very nice, is it?"

"I could see the signs," says Legend. "Once they start turning blue like that, it means only one thing. Mind you, in the circumstances I might have been a bit that way inclined myself. Know what I mean?"

Everybody nods silently.

"I mean, I knew a bloke once, found a geezer had been sending his old woman flowers. He had a nervous breakdown. Now, if you see your old lady sharing a pork sandwich with someone, that could really turn you off something rotten, couldn't it?"

Legend turns to me admiringly as the rank and vile waggle their heads up and down.

"I have to hand it to you, Lea. At first I thought you were some kind of poove, and even now I'm not sure, but, by Jiminy! You didn't half know how to say goodbye to old shagnasty, didn't you?"

I smile modestly. It is something I have been practicing for years and I am getting quite good at it now.

"Bloody unbelievable," continues Legend, patting me on the shoulder. "That woman seemed tight as a gnome's foreskin to me. How did you do it?"

"I don't know," I say, brushing imaginary dust from my forearms in order to cover my imaginary embarrassment. "It frightens me sometimes. Women just seem to go – well – sort of mad. I can't really put my finger on it."

"It's not your finger you have to worry about, is it?" says Legend who is no slouch in the wink, wink, nudge, nudge, department. I shrug my shoulders – they being all I have ever been capable of shrugging – and smile modestly at the envious inmates. "You must have had some times when you were making those films?"

"We all have our moments," I hear myself saying.

"Yours must stretch into years," says Grass admiringly.

"It's not all that fantastic," I tell him. "You get used to it after a bit and then it seems quite normal. You can even go off it. That's why I didn't fancy that bird you lined up for me, Arthur. Frankly, I was glad to get here for the rest."

Quite where I would have gone after that, I don't know, because one of the screws comes up and says that the Acting Governor wants to see me.

"Sure it isn't his old woman?" says one of the lags and the screw blushes. News of my little session with Mrs. Firm seems to have travelled faster than invitations to a Polynesian fertility rite.

"What's it all about then?" I ask as we pad down the corridors.

"Search me, but that bloke who's always on the telly is there."

"You mean Michael Aspel?"

"No, not him. The one who wants to clean up all the filth."

"Oh! Sir Ivor Bigun?"

"Yeah, that's right. I reckon he wants to see if he can get you put away for another stretch."

The screw looks about him to see if we are being observed and then draws closer. "Tell me, what were you doing to the Governor's old lady? Is it true that –"

"You don't want to believe everything you hear," I say hurriedly. "Now, let me see – It's this one, isn't it?"

I knock swiftly and bounce through the door into the ante room where the Governor's secretary is reading a paperback entitled "See Nipples And Die". She drops it into a drawer and looks at me disapprovingly before moving her minces over to the screw.

"2312763. Prisoner Lea for the A.G." he says conversationally.

Thrilled by my new found sensuality, I deliver a smouldering glance and wait hopefully for signs of smoke rising from the area of the knicker elastic. Not a sausage. Maybe she isn't wearing any. The quiet ones are the worst, you know.

"Go straight in," she says coldly. "He's expecting you."

The screw looks at her in some surprise as if he cannot understand why she is not clambering out of her dress and I click my tongue at her and push through the door.

The Acting Governor has about as much to distinguish him as a half-sucked lolly but Sir Ivor is instantly recognisable. He was the geezer, looking as if he went around smelling little girls' bicycle seats, who was at the première of "Revenge of the Creatures from the O.K. Corral" where I got pinched. The world, or that part of it that owns a T.V. set, knows him as president of the Fight Unclean Culture Korps, a society dedicated to: "Turning the insidious tide of pornography which is threatening to undermine the British way of life". Thanks to them and the stupid berk who spliced a bit of my privates' life into the film's action, I am where I am now.

"Let me come to the point at once, Lea," says the A.G., the minute I step through the door. "Sir Ivor, here, thinks you may be able to serve him."

This is asking a lot, I think to myself, but maybe there is more to come.

"Yes, Lea," says Bigun cutting across the A.G. like he is a rowing boat in front of the Q.E.II. "As you must know, I am responsible for producing a report on pornography in this country and it occurred to me and my committee that though we had made plans to examine all aspects of the sex industry, we did not actually have a representative from the industry on the panel. It struck me that this is something we should remedy and I have therefore asked the Home Secretary if he would be prepared to grant you parole on condition that you served with us and helped to produce the report. What do you say?"

Blimey! What can I say? "I wouldn't have to stay here?"

"Not if you were prepared to serve on the committee."
"Would I have to come back afterwards?"
"Your service would count as part of your sentence."
"Do I get paid?"
"No! ! Living expenses, that's all."
"Well," I pretend to be giving the matter some thought. "You think I'll be some use, do you?"
"Indubitably. Your inside knowledge will help us all tremendously. Every aspect of this ghastly traffic will be uncovered."
"We're doing something about traffic, are we?" I ask. "It's about time, too. You know, quite honestly, I reckon it's more important than the blue films. The other week it took me one and a half hours to get from Balham Tube Station to –"
"Not that kind of traffic!" snarls Sir Ivor, who does not look as if he has run up any outstanding bills at Charm School. "I mean, buying and selling corrupting material!"
"Oh, that. Yes, well, we'll want to cover that, won't we?"
The A.G. looks at Sir Ivor with a puzzled expression on his mush. "Are you sure this is the man you want?" he says.
Sir Ivor nods grimly. "Don't be deceived. Beneath this bluff, ingenuous exterior, lies a quagmire of depravity. The range and vileness of this man's activities defies the imagination."
The A.G. looks at me with a new respect.
"Give us a kiss," I say, pursing my lips at him.
"Steady, Lea," snaps Bigun. "Don't start taking liberties, my lad, or you'll soon be back behind bars."
"I'm sorry," I say humbly, "it was just the excitement of being free – I mean on parole."
"Yes, don't forget that you're only on parole. You'll have to work to make this secondment part of your sentence. You know what secondment means?"
"Is it the one after firstment?" I ask.
Somewhat to my surprise, I am told that I will be sent

home for a few days before meeting the rest of the committee and so, one fine morning, I find myself in Scraggs Lane outside the family pile, or haemmorhoid, as my mother would probably prefer to call it; she can be very refined sometimes. My departure from Penhurst has done little to diminish the legend that is building up around my name and only Warren, predictably seems to be bitter.

"You gay deceiver, you," he trills petulantly. "I thought you were my friend and now you turn your back on me."

"One of the few that dared," I say wittily, but he does not laugh. It must be his female hormones, I suppose.

Outside the ancestral home of the Leas I take a deep breath of soot and bang on the front door which sheds a few more leaves of peeling brown paint. There is a long pause and then the doors opens to reveal mum with her hands covered in flour and dough. This is a horrible sight because it means that she is baking a cake and my mum's cakes make old boots seem like flapjacks. When she hands you a plate of her buns and says "take your pick" she means it – literally.

If I had been in a really hard nick, I might have thought of getting her to send me a file baked in a cake, but it would have been useless – you could never have got the bastard out.

The minute she sees me, mum's mouth drops open and she looks past me into the street, up and down.

"Quick! Upstairs to the attic," she says.

"Hey. Steady on mum. You're getting flour all over my flying jacket."

"I don't care about that. Get upstairs before the police come. You were a fool to do it, and a bigger one to come here. Don't you know this is always the first place they look? If only you'd watched more 'Z Cars' when you were a kiddy, you wouldn't do things like that."

"Steady on, ma!" I say, trying to get her doughy fingers off me. "I haven't done a bunk. Straight up, I haven't. I'm on parole."

"What's that?" says mum suspiciously. "You haven't signed anything, have you?"

"No, no, I've got to help the government with a job."

"Not turning a nark, are you?" says mum reproachfully.

"No. One in the family is enough," I say bitterly, patting the stuffed moosehead which has now been moved to the humble hall of the Lea dwelling.

"Your father was only thinking of your long term good," says Mum loyally. "He thought a little stretch would do you good."

"I've often thought the same about him, mum," I say grimly. "Now come on, let's have a cup of tea. I haven't done a bunk, honest."

"You've chosen a good moment to come home," says mum, cheering up. "I'm making some rock cakes."

This is bad news for anyone interested in keeping a mouthful of teeth, so I ignore her words and press forward to the kitchen. It is no great surprise to find my rat fink father curled up with a cup of char next to the cooker. His disgusting nicotine-stained fingers are practically prising a bikini-clad lovely off the centre spread of the Sun – a paper dad has changed to from the Mirror because he admires its deep commitment to in depth reporting of crucial issues, its stand on ecology and the acres of semi-naked crumpet that are spread over nearly every page. When he sees me his face splits into a wide snarl of greeting.

"Come back to break your mother's heart, have you?" he says conversationally. "I'm amazed you dare show your face here."

"I'm amazed you dare show your face anywhere, dad," I say. "Still, I expect you get used to people laughing, after a while."

"Now, now, let's not have any unpleasantness," says mum moving in fast. "Timmy's home on parole, dear. That's nice, isn't it?"

The noise that escapes from Dad's lips might be called

a snort. "Nice? He heaps shame on our heads and you call it nice. I wouldn't mind so much if it was some kind of manly crime he'd committed. But getting mixed up with all that perversion. It gives the family a bad name. People are beginning to talk."

"I don't give a monkey what the old lags round here think," I say. "And I don't reckon I've done anything worse than you nicking all that stuff from the Lost Property Office. I suppose that's why you're at home so much. They've decided that because you've got most of the merchandise, they might as well operate from here." I am, of course, referring to the moosehead, forty-seven umbrellas, eighteen pairs of binoculars, fourteen tennis rackets, three stuffed owls and a cuspidor that makes the hall of the Lea mansion look like the reception area of a decrepid Highlands boarding house. Dad does not care for the tone of my remarks.

"Anything I bring home, I save from the incinerator. You know that as well as I do. So don't let's have any of your lip, Sonny Jim. I'd never stoop to appearing in an obscene photograph."

"What do you mean? I reckon any photograph with you in it is obscene."

"Now, that's not nice, dear," says Mum hurriedly. "You shouldn't talk to your father like that."

"Then why doesn't he get off my back, mum?" I yelp. "The minute I'm through the door, he's on at me. I wouldn't feel so bad about it if it hadn't been for his dirty magazines in the hallstand. You never owned up to that, did you, you dirty old deviant?! All that cobblers about obscene photographs and you spend your time getting a cheap thrill out of 'Danish Spanking Party'. Look at that paper. It's covered in drool stains. God knows what he's been up to, mother."

"I dropped my fried bread on it," whines dad. "Don't you listen to him, mother. He's trying to poison you against me."

"If I had any poison I wouldn't be wasting it on mum,"

I say bitterly. "You get right up my bracket, dad. Blood is supposed to be thicker than water, but I wouldn't reckon your lot above a bottle of red ink in Staines Reservoir."

Those familiar with the workings of the Lea household will realise that things are on the verge of getting out of hand. Fortunately, at that moment the front door bell whirrs and I escape to answer it.

Standing on the door step is a brown-skinned man of medium height bearing a faint resemblance to Paul Newman. He is accompanied by a browner version of my sister Rosie.

"Blimey!" says Sid. "You done a bunk, have you?"

"I'm on parole," I say. "I'll tell you about it later. Did you have a nice holiday?"

"Not bad," says Sid unenthusiastically shooting a swift glance at Rosie who's eyes appear to be elsewhere at the time. "Weather was nice."

"Unbelievable," says Rosie. She gives a soft, rhythmic shudder like a current running through thick cream and I wonder if she has been up to her tricks again. Rosie can be very naughty when the holiday spirit, e.g. brandy, gets her and experience has suggested that anyone born south of Haywards Heath turns her on like the Blackpool Illuminations. One or two incidents at a holiday village on the Isla de Amor and the Cromby Hotel at Hoverton have proved conclusively that the only way Rosie can get rid of temptation is by giving in to it.

"You didn't get bored, then?"

Sid shoots a glance at me – with a harpoon gun, I think. "What do you mean?"

"I mean – er, you didn't find that with just the two of you time hung on your hands?"

"We made some friends, didn't we, Sidney?" says Rosie cheerily.

"*You* made some friends," snarls Sid. "Look, do you want me to stand out here all morning or can we come in?"

Sidney's narky attitude suggests that my original surmise was right on the bollock. Rosie has obviously been giving the dagos a day out and Sidney is not exactly chuffed to NAAFI breaks about it.

"What are you doing here, then?" he grunts as we sweep past the handless barometer.

"I got out to serve on a committee investigating pornography," I tell him.

"Jammy bastard! You don't half know how to fall on your feet, don't you?"

"Don't encourage me to feed my fist up your hooter," I tell him. "If it hadn't been for you I wouldn't have got within five hundred miles of the chokey. I took the rap for –"

"All right, all right," snarls Sid. "Don't go on about it. I bet nobody else in the nick got out with you."

"You're a nice bloke, Sidney," I tell him. "You'd bash somebody's teeth out and then kick them in the goolies for mumbling."

"Oh, come off it, you two," trills Rosie fulfilling one of her many womanly roles. "It's like having dad here, listening to you two going on."

"Funny you should say that," I say with relish. "The miserable old sod basket is waiting to greet you at this very moment."

I fling open the kitchen door and there is Britain's best argument for euthanasia slurping down tea out of a saucer. It is a sight to make Barbara Cartland ring for the smelling salts.

"B-b-l-ooming heck," he splutters, setting up a miniature tidal wave that saturates the nude Sun cutie he is lapping up. "You two look like darkies. I wonder you got back in the country. Good job Enoch Powell didn't see you."

"Very jocular, dad," says Sidney. "Hello mum. How's it going?"

"Well as can be expected, dear. The old man has been a bit poorly lately."

"Ooh! That doesn't sound very nice. You want to lash out on a few monkey glands, dad."

"Yeah, but would you be prepared to part with them?" says dad who can be rude to anyone.

"Did you have a nice time, dear?" says Mum, diving in again.

"Oh it was lovely mum. Lovely hotel. Lovely weather. The food was nice. At least, I thought it was nice. Sidney picked up some bug –"

"Huh!!" snorts Sidney. "I picked up some bug. If we're going to start about picking up bugs, I'd like to ask you what you think that long-haired creep who spent his mornings sweeping the bottom of the swimming bath was?"

"Oh, no! Do we have to go through that again?" sighs Rosie. "Honest, mum, he's so insanely jealous I have to put on a pair of gloves before I can give the bus conductor the fare. He'd like to chain me up at home and never let me look at another man."

"Looking is all right," says Sid. "You look a bit close sometimes."

"And what does that mean? What are you trying to say?! The only way your evil little mind gets any exercise is by jumping to conclusions."

"Oh, for gawd's sake!" I say. "Belt up the lot of you! It's a bloody sight more restful back in the nick."

"Don't swear, dear," says mum. "I don't like to hear you when you swear."

I should be touched because mum still cares whether I swear or not. She does not give a bugger about dad and Sidney.

"That's right, you tell him, ma," squeaks Rosie. "He always was prone to bad language."

"You're a fine one to talk about being prone," snarls Sidney who obviously has been through a very harrowing experience – amongst a lot of other things. That remark goes down about as well as a pork pie taste test at a barmitzvah and I nip out to the khasi and read through the cut up pieces of the T.V. Times that take the place of bog paper in the Lea throne room. Funny how it is much more interesting when you have to skip about a bit to keep track of an article. Like when you sit in a train and see some other bloke reading a newspaper you have finished five minutes before. Suddenly every headline you see seems fascinating and you can never remember having seen it before.

I am so absorbed in reading about what the stars wish their pets in 1974 that I set to work with a piece of paper that still has a staple in it. Sensitive readers will not need any help from me in imagining the effect achieved by this act of diabolical incompetence on my penny-paring mother's part, and I hobble out into the yard – or back garden as my mum calls it, feeling that I will not be passing this way again for a long time.

As I emerge, Sidney is enjoying a quiet drag outside the kitchen door and he looks me up and down suspiciously.

"Nobody had a go at you while you were inside, did they?" he asks.

"What do you mean?!" I say indignantly.

"Well, the way you're walking it looks as if you've found a new way of smuggling bananas."

"Get out of it! I did myself an injury on a staple mum left in the bog paper. I'm no more bent than you are."

"Steady on, steady on," soothes Sidney. "I can see you're in a bad mood. There's no need to take it out on me."

Sidney is always much happier if he can diagnose everybody else as suffering from his ailment and he is not slow to throw out a few "for whys" as well.

"Frustration," he says. "That's your trouble, isn't it? Cooped up in there without sight nor sound of a bird. Can't be good, can it?"

"Well, actually –" I begin, but Sid does not let me get very far.

"You don't have to explain," he continues. "I've done my bird, haven't I? I know what it's like. I remember the first bint I had when I came out. She didn't know what hit her."

"Came up behind her in a dark alley, did you, Sid?"

"Don't take the piss. I'm talking about passion, aren't I?"

"I suppose so, Sid," I say. I am thinking about my last day in the nick. Mrs. Sinden's old man had been sent off on a course and I was collecting her dirty laundry from half past eight until five o'clock. Not only that, but I was responsible for getting most of it dirty, too. Blimey! What a performer. I have heard of people bending over backwards to get on the stage but she could bend in about fifteen different directions at once. And – as for appetite – fantastic! I think she had a waste disposal unit between her legs. She could churn up anything you cared to offer her and lie back waiting for more. When I left her quarters I was practically in eighths. I went over the front doorstep like a jelly rolling down the up escalator. All in all, Sidney could not be more wrong about my present condition, which resembles that of a bowl of brawn waiting to set. Nevertheless, he continues to rabbit on.

"I know what you need," he says, patting me on the shoulder. "A bit of the other – and pronto!" I suppress a shudder which he does not notice and shrug my shoulders non-commitally.

"I don't think –" I begin.

"You don't have to think," says Sid, lowering his voice confidentially. "I've done all the thinking."

"What do you mean, Sid?"

"I mean I've laid it on for you, haven't I? While you've been sitting here scratching your arse, I've been making a couple of telephone calls. I'm organising a welcome home party."

"What? At Scraggs Lane?"

"No! The only thing your dad would welcome home is a first divi. This place has got about as much homely atmosphere as the inside of an abandoned refrigerator."

"Where, then?"

"One of my mates. Do you remember Frank Peppard?"

"Oh yeah. The geezer who had so many spots we used to call him Peppard the Leopard?"

"That's him. He's got a flat above the Plough now."

"You mean the boozer that used to be called the Brown Cow?"

"That's right. You've heard of 'How now, brown cow'? Well it's 'Brown Cow, now Plough'."

"Oh, Sidney, please! Do us a favour!"

I mean, it is diabolical, isn't it? It is bad enough listening to your own lousy jokes, without your poxy brother-in-law getting in on the act.

"Yeah. Clever that, isn't it?" Sidney's bonce bounces up and down like it is on a piece of elastic.

"Fantastic, Sid. Quite fantastic. Look, this geezer Peppard. I can't imagine him giving much of a party."

"Oh, he's changed. He's had injections for his spots and he fills the holes up with make-up so the birds don't notice until he's on the job, and by then it's too late."

"You mean the holes from the injections?"

"No, you berk! I mean, where the spots were. He's really a very nice looking fella these days."

"I'm very happy for him, Sid. Well, it really is very nice of you to fix me up like this." It is, isn't it? Too nice, for Sidney, somehow. "What's in it for you?" I ask. Sidney flashes on his "oh, you've noticed" expression.

"Well, I'll be coming along, won't I?"

"With Rosie, of course?"

"Won't be her cup of tea, will it?" says Sid, winking at me. "Frank's got a few bits of skirt lined up that get headaches if they don't have it three times a day. Do you remember Avis Figgins?"

"No," I say gratefully.

"She's a goer, that one. I'm surprised you don't remember her. A bit before your time, I suppose. I keep forgetting you were a perishing virgin when I first met you."

Virgin! It is like a dirty word to me. I cringe every time I hear it. I can never imagine myself being a virgin.

It is like being told that your balls did not drop out of your bum until you were ten.

"That's a long time ago, Sid."

It is obvious from the "where's my drool cup" expression on Sidney's mush that our boy reckons he is in for a feature or two. No doubt his sun-soaked holiday with Miss Hot Pants has left him with a few old scores to pay off.

"When's the big event?" I ask. "I'm only home for the weekend."

"Tonight," says Sid with grim satisfaction. "You haven't got anything laid on, have you?"

"Not yet, Sid. No." Actually, I was thinking of turning in early with a mug of milky Ovaltine, but I do not want to let on to Sid that I am not feeling up to it.

"Well, don't bother," says Sid. "The birds tonight guarantee more bangs than a box of crackers."

I smile weakly and try to look enraptured rather than enruptured.

"Thanks, Sid," I mutter. "I don't know what to say." It is the truth. I don't.

"That's all right, Timmo." Sid claps me on the back. "Just don't make too much of a pig of yourself, that's all. The girls all know you're coming."

I wish I did, I think to myself. Blimey, I wonder where mum keeps the malt extract these days.

All through the rest of the day I am worrying about it and by late afternoon I would be pushed to make a dent in a plate of cold soup. You must know the feeling. The more you think about it, the more you can feel your J.T. turning in to a strip of parboiled spaghetti. You can never imagine getting it into a straight line again. I have half decided to pretend to be ill and skip the whole thing when I remember Dad's dirty book collection in the hall-stand. Maybe there will be some inspiration there. Some frisky frolicking that will graft some muscle on to mopey Dick. I dive into the debris and sure enough, there is a tattered tome entitled "Over 44". At first glance I think this must refer to the age of the birds featured. By the cringe! What a load of old scrubbers! But a closer glance indicates that it must mean their knocker measurements. I like a nicely turned bristol as well as the next man but you can have too much of a good thing. Most of them would be pushed to get their tits in a couple of policeman's helmets. All in all, it is doing less than nothing for Percy. In fact, it is making me feel even more choked with the whole idea.

It is in this mood of black depression that my eye falls upon an advertisement at the back of the magazine.

"Men! Do you have a problem? Do you always deliver the goods? With New Wonder Stallion you can make all the girls happy, all the time. Just depress the plunger and Stallion takes over where your libido leaves off. When you use Stallion, she won't be able to say neigh!!"

Well, I don't usually go in for that kind of thing, but maybe, in the circumstances, I had better give it a whirl. Trouble is that the stuff is sent to you by post under a plain cover and I want it tonight. "Hepditch Laboratories, Hepditch Road." That is just round the corner! At least, Hepditch Road is. I cannot remember Hepditch Laboratories. Number 43 it says here. I had better pop round and get some. My bike is still in the shed but the tyres are flatter than Twiggy's kid sister so I pad round to Hepditch Road on foot. On both sides of the street is an unbroken line of terraced houses and I don't know where the laboratories come in. Number 43 looks like number 41 and not particularly unlike number 39. Maybe the windows are a bit dirtier, that's all. I ring the bell which does not seem to work and am about to chuck it in and go down with 'flu when the door flies open and a nasty looking old slag heap flashes her peepers up and down me. Her fag has more ash than tobacco and her housecoat looks as if it was used to mop up after a meths drinkers coffee morning.

"Whadderyerwant?" she demands.

"Is this Hepditch Laboratories?"

"Umph." This remark could be taken as meaning "yes" or "that depends".

"I want to buy some Stallion," I say lowering my voice discretely. I mean, it is not the kind of thing you want everyone to know about, is it?

"Stallion?" shouts the miserable old rat bag so that everybody in the street must be able to hear her. " I don't know if we've got any left. Hang on a minute, I'll just ask the chief pharmacist. HENREEE!!!" She turns her back on me and bawls up the stairs. "Have we got any number forty seven? That's right." There is a muffled shout from above and she turns back to me. "Impotence, isn't it?"

"Temporary," I whisper urgently. "Temporary."

"Temporary impotence!!" screeches the crone. "What? Oh, is it?" She turns back to me. "It's the same stuff."

"All right, all right." I breathe. "How much do I owe you?"

"You want some, do you? You must be in a hurry."

She peers past me into the street as if expecting to see some bird lying in the gutter with her legs apart. "We do all our stuff by post, usually."

"I just happen to be passing," I hiss. "Now, how much is it?"

"Three pounds fifty."

"Three pounds fifty!"

"You're saving on postage."

"O.K." It seems diabolical but I would rather pay the money and get the hell out of it.This place gives me the creeps. I fumble in my wallet and shagnasty retreats to the foot of the stairs and reappears with a cap of aerosol spray. The label, hurriedly stuck on it, says "Stallion – for men – plus!"

"It really works, does it?" I ask, wishing I had my mouth shut the second I have spoken.

"Do you want to try it?" leers the horrible old bag.

"I'll take your word for it," I say hurriedly, and head for home.

Later that evening I am tripping up the stairs beside

the saloon bar of the Plough and the Stallion is making a reassuring bulge in the pocket of my jeans. It is not the only thing either. Hepditch Laboratories brainchild really does seem to work. I have only given the aerosol a little squeeze but the effect has been instantaneous and impressive. A sensation not unlike frostbite of the hampton followed by more growth than is normally prophesied in a unit trust advertisement. And permanent growth to boot. Percy has refused to fold up for travel and getting my flared denims on has been like storing away an ironing board without collapsing it.

"Hey, wait a minute! I know you, don't I?"

The geezer squinting at me is vaguely recognisable from the distant past and is a good deal plumper than he probably likes to think of himself as being.

"Yeah of course. Rosie's kid brother, isn't it? How is she? Still –"

"Yes," I say hurriedly. "She's fine. Married to Sid Noggett. Is he around anywhere?"

"Not yet. He's giving one or two of the birds a lift. Not for the first time, eh?"

I acknowledge his wit with a brave smile and extend an arm. "Timothy Lea."

"Frank Peppard. Pleased to meet you again. Yeah, Sid told me all about you. The party's in your honour, isn't it? We've got one or two right ravers lined up."

Peppard draws me to one side and whispers in my ear. "I wouldn't tell anyone this but there's a little room just beyond the kitchen. You'll be all right in there if you see anything you fancy. I know how you must feel."

"Thanks," I murmur, wondering what brand of B.O. Frank uses.

"Don't mensh. The lock turns anti-clockwise. Just put everything back vaguely as you'd like to find it."

"Thanks." I am looking past Peppard into the interior of the flat. Already there is a fair sprinkling of birds and the Tamla Motown is slurping round your knees like crotch treacle. What a shame I am feeling less like nooky than pulling my foreskin over my head and whistling "Rule, Britannia". My action man kit still seems as dead as a drugged toothy-peg, but a glance at the home of the y-front reveals that Percy continues to be rigor mortis locked. Maybe I will be able to have a few drinks and keep out of trouble.

"How do you fancy that one?" says Peppard pointing out a dumpy little bird with big eyes, tits, feet, arms, shoulders – you name it – it's all big.

"Very nice," I say, "but I've always reckoned slim birds myself."

"You want Gail, then; look at her arse. It's like a couple of grapes in a sausage skin isn't it?"

"Yeah – she's lovely. But a bit on the tall side for me. I don't like birds that come above shoulder height."

"Depends how often they come, doesn't it?"

Peppard kills himself laughing and I think of all the ways I would have preferred him to do the job.

"Very good," I say, to make him put a sock in it. "Do you think I could have a drink?"

"Yeah, of course," he says, a bit surprised. "Funny, but I thought you'd be leaping at a chance to get your end away after all this time."

"Oh, I am. But I'm very fussy. They have to be just right before I fancy them."

"That's not what Sidney said."

"No? Well, he doesn't know everything."

I accept a glass of light ale and no sooner has the froth coated my lips than the man himself staggers through the door with a bird hanging on to each arm. When you see what he is trying to do with his hands you can see why they are hanging on.

"Timmo!" he squeals covering the front of my pearl-buttoned, pre-shrunk, blue faded denim shirt with a fine rain of spit. "How's it going, then? What's the score?!!!"

"No score, Sidney. Play hasn't started yet."

"Don't leave it too long, Timmo. Here, meet the girls.

This is Cilla and this is Trixie. I've told them all about you, haven't I girls?"

"Yeah. Now you want to tell us your side," says Trixie, digging her elbow into me. Marvellous, isn't it? Everybody you bump in to is a comedian these days.

"Don't be like that, Trix," says the other one seriously. "I think it's awful, cooping people up like that. It must be terribly bad for your nervous system not being able to lead a normal life."

"She means sex life," says Trixie, making with the elbow again. "That's all she thinks about!"

"Ooh, you fibber! You know I never."

"You do!"

"I never!"

"Don't listen to her," murmurs Sidney moving to my side. "She's got a faster action than a repeating rifle, that one. Damn near had it out on the way over here."

"Straight up?"

"You never said a truer word. Get in there, boy. You'll be doing her a favour."

"I don't know, Sid. I've got a bit of a headache."

"What's the matter with you?! Frank and I have gone to a lot of trouble to line this lot up for you. Are you trying to insult us or something?" Sid looks at me closely. "You sure you haven't turned bent in there? They can give you electric shock treatment, you know."

"I'll bear it in mind, Sid. No, it's just that – oh well. It doesn't matter. I expect I'll feel better in a minute."

"Yeah. Well, if I was in your position, I know what position I'd be in. Get me?"

"Yes Sid."

"Well don't just stand there. Ask her to dance. Blimey, you're worse than when I first met you."

So I grab Cilla and give her a line of chat that would make a party political broadcast a white hot contender for the top L.P. spot. But the stupid bird does not get the message. She goes rabbiting on about what I have been missing while I was in the nick. "I don't know how often other people do it," she trills, "but I think I'd go mad if I didn't have sexual relations a couple of times a week. I mean, don't get me wrong, I don't believe in making love on your first date – not unless you're really fond of each other, that is. After all, it is 1973 –"

"Is it?" I say, looking at my watch. "Blimey, I'd better be –"

"I'm not embarrassing you, am I? I mean, I think you can talk about these things these days, don't you?"

"Yes," I say wearily. "I'm blooming positive of it. Would you like a glass of fruit cup? If you hold the orange peel out of the way I can – oh bugger!"

Some berk has poured his drink down the front of my jeans. This is definitely not one of my big evenings.

"Come into the kitchen," says Cilla eagerly. "I'll sponge it dry for you."

"Hello, hello, hello," says Frank.

"How much did you give him to do that?" says Sid.

With both of them giving thumbs up signs as we go into the kitchen I reckon I might as well chuck in the sponge. If I don't go through with it everybody is going to be narky and my reputation will be lower than a dachshund's balls. A quick stab of the Stallion should give me enough horsepower to do the job.

The cannister is tucked in the top of my jeans and I remove it as we enter the kitchen. Cilla grabs a tea towel. "Lucky it wasn't red wine," she says.

"Yeah," I pop the aerosol onto the work surface behind me and try to stop her rubbing the teeth out of the zip on my flies.

"Hey! Steady on. I might want to use that some time."

"Is that a threat or a promise?" She snuggles up to me and peels open her sticky lips. I must be in a bad way because the sight interests me less than Ted Heath tap dancing on wet suet.

"Do you want to go next door? We could be alone there."

"Smashing." I allow her to take my hand and am half

way through the door before I remember the Stallion. "Hold on a minute. I'll just get my drink." I sweep the aerosol down to my side and keep it hidden as we enter a room so small that the door practically scuffs the opposite wall when you open it.

"Intimate, isn't it?" she says.

"Blimey! I'll say. Where's the khasi?"

"Don't say things like that. I'm feeling all romantic."

She starts rubbing herself against me and it is a cast-iron certainty that she is not mentally recataloguing her stamp collection. I pop the Stallion into a shadowy alcove and prepare to send Willy out to work.

A settee about as low as Cilla's mind takes up most of the room and she sinks onto it pulling me with her.

"Take your jeans off," she says. "They'll dry easier. Oh, you poor boy. You've almost forgotten what it's like, haven't you?"

She starts assaulting me with her lips and her ferret fingers plunder the front of my jeans like they are trying to pluck out the stitches. This girl may not be the most beautiful thing I have ever laid hands on but for eagerness she is England Football Squad material. Sir Alf Ramsey would really respond to her brand of whole-hearted get up and go – or get it up and stay, more likely.

Percy is responding with all the mad irrepressible enthusiasm of a rusty clockwork snake fed on lazy beans and my hand sneaks out for the Stallion. Summoning up the last couple of ounces of passion left over from another occasion I motor down on Cilla's lips with sufficient force to press her back onto the bed. Her arms slide round my body and I pull down the front of my pants and drag the unwilling Percy into the open. Now, for the magic transformation scene. One squirt of Stallion and – Shazam!!! Mini Mouse turns into King Rat. I reach behind me, close my fingers round the aerosol and –

YEEE-O-O-O-O-W!!!

My feet do not touch the floor as I zoom off the bed and through to the kitchen. A small knot of people are standing about eating bits of cheese and they look up with something approaching interest as I burst between them with my hampton in my hands. This article looks like an over-boiled frankfurter and feels as if someone has just dunked it in sulphuric acid. I turn the tap full on and start swilling water over it from an empty milk bottle.

"What's happened?" says Sid appearing in the doorway whilst girls scream and men either laugh or make threatening noises.

I don't have time to answer because Cilla comes out of the bedroom holding the aerosol in her hand.

"He's mad!" she says. "He just squirted his thing with oven scourer!"

CHAPTER SIX

I don't know what they put in those oven scourers but they don't contain a lot of hand cream, I can tell you. I had visions of my old man ending up like a still-born mouse. I spent the next two days in the local swimming baths and the attendant got dead worried wondering why I stood in the shallow end reading a book from the minute the bath opened till closing time. That was the best part of my day. The nights were agony. They are never very good at Scraggs Lane at the best of times but when you cannot park your hampton anywhere without suffering instant agony there is not a lot of shut-eye flitting about.

It is not until the Monday morning that things start to get a little better and that is when I have to meet Sir Ivor and the rest of the Committee.

Mum looks me up and down very suspicious like as I limp to the breakfast table.

"You've been walking funny ever since you came out of that place," she says.

"Not just walking," says Sid. "I don't know what they've done to him in there but he's a bit peculiar all round, if you ask me."

"Give it a rest, will you, Sid?" I plead.

"He seems to want to inflict pain on himself all the time," continues my poxy brother-in-law. "It's all very kinky, if you ask me."

"I've read about it," says Mum, who is always quick to believe the worst of me. "You haven't fallen into bad company, have you dear?"

"Don't be ridiculous, mum. I was born into it and married into it. What's the difference if I suddenly start falling into it?"

"Masochists. That's what they are called," says Sid

grimly. "They get their sexual kicks out of being hurt. I read about it at the dentist's."

"Very appropriate place, Sid. I expect you get a lot of them down there, begging for the drill instead of a mouth wash."

"Don't take the piss, Timmy. I'm dead serious about this. You're not the same, carefree bloke you used to be."

"Deep down inside I am. Don't you worry. Underneath the third degree burns I'm the same starry-eyed little kid with a song on his lips and a good word for everybody. In fact, Sidney, as far as you're concerned I've got a very good word for you right now." Fortunately, I do not use it but relations between me and the family are definitely strained and I am not sorry to be tripping away down Scraggs Lane towards the bus stop. That vehicle, with the help of a couple of its large red friends carries me to a tasty little address round the back of St. James's Park. You cannot move without falling over a taxi and everybody is wearing a bowler hat and an expression as if someone has shoved a clothes peg up their hooter. I ring the doorbell, which is so large I can see my face in it, and take in the gold-topped railings and the horse lamps. Must be nice to have a few bob.

The door opens and a butler-type geezer looks me up and down and sucks in his breath sharply. Maybe my blue suede flying jacket with the lambs wool trim was not a good idea. "Ye-es?" he says as if he would much rather be saying "no-o!"

"Sir Ivor is expecting me," I say grandly. "Lea is the name. Timothy Lea."

"Follow me, ple-ease," says the butler resigning himself to the worst. "The others are upstairs."

I am screwing myself into a rare state of anticipation as I pad up the semi-circular marble staircase, so I hardly look at all the paintings and the gilt bits and pieces on the walls. It seems more like a museum than a private house.

"Sir Ivor lives here?" I ask.

"Amongst other places," says the funky flunkey, coldly.

My old man gives a twinge as I go through the high carved doors so my expression is not vastly different from those I meet on the other side of it – pained and preoccupied. Besides Sir Ivor, there is a wizened little man with round shoulders and eyes like gimlets, and two birds.

"Birds" is not a very good description unless you immediately think of vultures. They are both wearing black as if seldom out of it and their skirt length makes quite sure that they do not give any cheap thrills to knee fetishists. If they are wearing bras they are of the kind that are only there in case their owners get involved in a road accident and their faces are scrubbed a healthy shade of pink. Age-wise, they must be at the wrong end of the thirties. The raw material is not bad but the presentation suggests that they would be pushed to shove a bunch of flowers in a vase of water the right way up.

Sir Ivor moves to greet me and I can see him struggling with himself whether to shake hands with me or not. He decides against it and holds up a hand for the silence he already has.

"Ah hah!" he chortles. "The man we have all been waiting for. Our agent from the underworld: Timothy Lea. Helen, let me introduce Timothy Lea: Miss Helen Golly."

The bird has a handsome mane of black hair, most of it sprouting from her upper lip and thick rimless specs that look like half-sucked lolly pops. Her lips are diabolically sensual and glisten moistly.

"Charmed," I say, extending my hand eagerly.

"How do you do," she says, ignoring it.

"And Amanda: Timothy Lea. Timothy Lea: Amanda Pumps."

"Née Rumbold," she says.

For a moment I think she has said "Neigh Rumbold". She is definitely that kind of girl. Big horsey teeth, and a snozz to match. A real nose bag, in fact.

What a couple of little darlings. I wonder what they do out of the pantomime season.

"Pleased to meet you."

"How do you do."

She looks me up and down like the housemaid has just scraped me off the nursery carpet, and I wish I was back in clink again. It is women like her who get pornography a bad name.

"Amanda and Helen are lay women," says Sir Ivor.

Well, you could have fooled me. I would not have reckoned that those two birds had ever seen an unsheathed pork bayonet, let alone had the pleasure of one. Still, you can never tell. Maybe Amanda did not get those teeth from trying to eat a piece of cheese through a keyhole.

"Professor Hans Joddrell is, of course, the noted Danish Sexologist. You are no doubt acquainted with the synopsis of his work that has appeared in the popular press?"

Now that he mentions it I do recall the Sunday Filth running a serialisation of Joddrell's book "The Ape Within Us" full of startling revelations about things I had always taken for granted. I look at the wizened old geezer with a fresh interest.

"I have seen your film," he says wistfully. "That is real pornography, I think."

I shrug, Helen shudders and Amanda makes an exclamation of disgust.

"We can come back to that later," says Sir Ivor briskly. "I'm afraid that before we get down to serious work we have the formality of the press. Whilst much preferring that we could undertake our work in camera, so to speak, I am certain that you can all appreciate the benefits to our cause of focussing public attention on the fight against filth. For that reason I have asked a few gentlemen of the press here so that we can explain to them our aims and let the world at large know what we are doing."

"What about misrepresentation?" says Amanda.

"Is she on the committee, too?" I ask, getting all excited.

"I didn't know we were having beauty queens. I thought Eric Morley had them all tied up."

"Please, Lea," says Sir Ivor, rolling his eyes round the ceiling. "Control yourself." He turns to Amanda Pumps.

"Some misrepresentation is inevitable, I'm afraid," he says. "But if we believe in what we are doing, we must harden ourselves against it."

"Get a hard on," I say helpfully.

"I've heard that expression," says Helen Golly brightly. "I never knew what it meant before. Yes, let's all get a hard on."

"You will find it exceptionally difficult," observes Joddrell drily. "It refers to the male organ becoming swollen with blood prior to intercourse taking place."

"Ooh! How disgusting!" squeaks Amanda.

"Perhaps. But inevitable," shrugs Joddrell. "No alternative method has proved as effective."

"I won't tell you again, Lea," hissed Sir Ivor. "One more uncalled for remark and I will have you returned to prison forthwith."

The way he says it he could even mean thirdwith.

"Will they want to take photographs?" says Amanda wrinkling up her hooter.

Not once they see you, I think to myself, but I am wrong. When another pair of doors are flung open, the press can hardly wait to put down their large gin and tonics before snapping everything that moves. I notice that Sir Ivor is not slow to hog the lens and that a copy of "The Ape Within Us" appears like magic in Hans Joddrell's mole-like mitts. The ladies are more retiring.

"Would you mind crossing your legs, Miss Pumps?" huffs one snap dragon.

"I thought they were crossed," says another.

"No. You're getting confused with her eyes," says Number One.

"Come on, Miss Pumps. Give us a bit of allure. Show us you know what you're up against."

"I wouldn't think she's been up against anything, poor old thing. That's her trouble."

"Yeah. It's a shame, isn't it? Come on darling. Give me a smile. No. On second thoughts –"

Helen is proving no more co-operative and I cannot see Hugh Hefner keeping his July centre spread open much longer.

"Tell me, Miss Golly, is it true that you refuse to wear coloured underwear?"

"How dare you!"

"Would you mind turning this way a bit. Great! And just moving your –"

"How dare you! Keep your hands to yourself, you jackanapes!" The bloke staggers back nursing his jaw and I have to concede that I have seldom seen such a mean right hand on anyone fighting at her weight.

"Gentlemen! Please! Let's have some decorum," purrs Sir Ivor, stepping away from a painting of a bunch of religious geezers with halos, pointing at just where he was standing. "Channel your questions through me, please. Let us have no sensationalism."

"How is your committee going to operate?" asks a red-headed geezer with a pipe clamped between his teeth.

"Our conviction is that pornography is directly responsible for undermining moral standards and for an unwarrantable increase in anti-social activities. It will be the business of our committee to build up evidence that this is indeed the case and to put forward recommendations for containing the spread of this cancer."

"Bring back the birch!" yelps Amanda Pumps looking at me longingly.

"You believe in corporal punishment?" says another reporter eagerly. The pencils are poised.

"I'm convinced it's the only thing a hardened pornographer understands. Those who deal in flesh should be punished through the flesh."

"I totally disagree," sniffs Helen Golly, pushing back her specs. "It is only by getting inside the mind of the pornographer that you will change him. Pornography is a mental sickness that cannot be cured by brute force."

"But –"

"As you see, we have a healthy divergence of views amongst our committee members," beams Bigun moving in with Elliot Ness swiftness. "Nobody could accuse us of having made up our minds before starting. We even have a convicted pornographer to ensure a totally balanced viewpoint." He waves a hand at me and everybody takes a good look at a convicted pornographer. I see a faint glow of envy kindle itself in the corner of one or two eyes.

"Very nice," says one of the cameramen. "Tell you what would make a very nice photograph. If you two girls would go and sit on the gentleman's lap –"

"No! !" hiss Amanda and Helen simultaneously.

"Well, supposing he sat on your –"

"No! !"

"Gentlemen, please!" interjects Sir Ivor. "How many times do I have to remind you of the serious purpose of our work? These ladies are not here to provide you with pin-up material."

An ugly, snorting laugh rings out from the back of the room and everybody, including the man who laughed, turns round questioningly before Sir Ivor continues. "Now, if there are no more serious questions, I will close the conference. A printed statement of our aims is available for you to take away with you."

"Where are you going to start?" asks Copper-Nut.

"Prostitution," says Sir Ivor. "We will be talking to a number of these unfortunate women and attempting to discover what effect exposure to pornography had on their choice of career."

"Do you know many prostitutes?" says a reporter, hopefully.

Sir Ivor shakes his head, and the pens sink down towards the pads again.

"We are well aware of the methods used by these ladies

to advertise their services and we will be making our contacts via them."

He nods at me as if seeking confirmation that this is the best method of contacting tarts and I nod back. Not that I know much about it. The only tart I can remember is Sid's Aunty Lil on Clapham Common, way back in my pre-nooky days, and that was an experience – or lack of it – that still sends cold shivers up and down my y-fronts.

"What do you think about this enterprise, Herr Joddrell?" asks a serious-looking journalist cove.

"Well, I think I have made my position clear in my book 'The Ape Within Us'. Available from all good class bookshops or direct by post from –"

"Yes, yes," says Sir Ivor. "I think we can say that our good friend Hans will be making his own inimitable contribution to our work. And now, if there are no more questions –"

He rambles on a bit and I become aware that Amanda has moved to my side and is gazing earnestly into my face. Her lower lip is trembling.

"I saw that film," she says. "It was unspeakable."

"You mean 'Monster from the O.K. Corral'? Yes, it was bad, wasn't it? I think they were fools to try and combine the two kinds of movie. And, of course, the location didn't help. I mean, Wanstead Marshes –"

"I was referring to the explicit sexual content," hisses Amanda. "You. Writhing with those naked women. Flaunting your brute male sensuality." She licks her lips and flares her nostrils. "Disgusting!"

"How did you manage to see it? That version didn't go out on release. In fact, none of the film got released; it escaped."

"Sir Ivor secured it for us. I was horrified. How could any woman be persuaded to do such things to a man? To debase herself like an animal. Prostrate herself before him and –"

"Please!" I yelp. "You're hurting!" I am not kidding. She has sunk her nails into my forearm and is squeezing me with a force I might have described as passionate had it been applied by someone else. She looks down at my arm as if seeing it for the first time and flings it aside.

"Voluptuary," she hisses. "Animal! Beast! Brute! Satyr! Despoiler of young girls! If you think you're going to add me to your list you've got another think coming." She gives a long shudder and turns on her heel. What a funny woman! I am no psychologist, but I do not reckon she is as anti a spot of the other as she makes out to be. I have read about women like her.

No sooner has she disappeared in search of a glass of carrot juice than I feel another hand on my arm. This time the touch is gentle and I look down into Helen Golly's misty minces.

"I'm sorry I was a trifle brusque when we first met," she says. "I was still a little overcome by your screen persona." I nod understandingly though I don't really understand.

"What I said about the relationship between pornography and mental illness must have seemed rather offensive, too."

"Don't let it worry you," I assure her. "I don't really think of myself as a pornographer."

"That's very interesting," she says. "Very interesting. We must talk more about all this. I'd like to try and get inside you."

Well, you can't say fairer than that, can you? I might feel the same if it was not for that blooming moustache guarding her cakehole. Somehow I can never really go a bundle on hairy birds. I blurt out a few words which more or less add up to a sentence and she pads off into the thinning ranks of the press. Now that the hard stuff seems to have been replaced by cups of coffee they are disappearing faster than snow drops in a blast furnace. I am about to try and detect the source of the alcoholic refreshment when I am accosted by a striking blonde lady wearing a fur wrap and an expression that looks as if it has shot searching glances into the inside of more than a few million martini glasses.

"How about an exclusive quickie?" she snaps.

"I thought you'd never ask," I say, flashing my pearlies at her in the approved Bogart fashion.

"I'm talking about an interview."

"I couldn't go on living in this dream for the rest of my life, could I?"

"My name is Greta Starkers. You may have heard of my column."

"I should have done. It sounds a real breakthrough. Isn't your husband jealous?"

If Miss Starkers thinks that I am a laugh riot she is not letting on to anyone about it.

"I thought it might be a good idea to interview you for my paper," she says. "But I'm prepared to have second thoughts about it."

Of course, I have heard of Greta Starkers. Well, everyone has, haven't they? She is the fearless, outspoken, tell-it-like-it-is, no-nonsense, warm, human, homely, sophisticated, frank, abrasive, scared of nothing except falling circulation, female columnist of the Morning Press. She has her finger on the issues that matter in the world we live in and, I notice, shapely knockers to boot – not that I like booting shapely knockers, I hasten to add. I have my funny little ways like all of us, but that is not amongst them.

"I'll be right with you. Hey, Jeeves," I grab Bigun's butler by the sleeve. "Could you find me a drink that isn't made from natural fruit juice or coffee beans? Thanks. Now, Miss Starkers. I'm all yours. And anything left over is yours as well."

Miss S. is by no means unappealing and it is a pity that Percy is still suffering from the effects of the oven scourer. This girl might stop at nothing to get a story and this is what I would normally put in her way.

"Do we have to talk here?" she says. "I favour something more intimate myself. What are you doing for lunch?"

"Testing a couple of strait jackets. Nothing I can't get out of."

"Did they put you in prison for making jokes like that, or was there something else?"

"Raping women reporters," I say. "Excuse me a moment, I must have a word with Sir Ivor." I move swiftly to the great man's side. He is adjusting his tie in the mirror and you can see that it was love at first sight.

"Miss Starkers wants to interview me over lunch," I say. "Is that all right? I'll be very careful what I say."

"You'd better be," snaps Bigun. "I'll be studying that rag of hers with a magnifying glass. One comment out of place, my lad and it's back to Penhurst."

"Thanks," I say. "I'll bear that in mind."

I avoid the unpleasant look in his eyes and trip back to Miss Starkers.

"O.K." I say. "Where are we going?"

"I've just remembered I'm on a diet," she says. "Why don't we go back to my place? I have a Filipino houseboy who can run up something."

"Like a flight of stairs?" I sniff. "I might have guessed there'd be a catch in this."

"He's a most marvellous cook," assures Miss S. "You should see his testimonials."

"Are you sure it won't put me off my food?"

"How long a sentence were you serving?" beams Miss Starkers. "I'd like to organise a petition to get it extended."

When we get outside there is a green Jag waiting and a bloke in a chauffeur's uniform to tear the door open. He looks at me and smiles a bit old-fashioned like. I am not certain I like what he is thinking.

"Back to the flat, Mainwaring," she says. "Now, Mr. Lea. Tell me something about yourself. When did you first decide you wanted to be a pornographer?"

"When I saw a pattern for camiknickers in my mother's sewing basket."

"Do you have any regrets?"

"It's a very misunderstood profession. I didn't even understand I was in it until I went to a film première one day." I explain to her what happened and by that time we are pulling up outside a tall red brick house off Kensington High Street.

"Wait here, Mainwaring," she says. "I won't be too long."

Mainwaring shakes his head and smiles to himself in a way that suggests he has heard all that before, and leans back, tipping his peaked cap over his eyes.

"He comes with the job, does he?" I ask.

"Slightly less seldom than that, I think," says Miss S. drily. "Come and meet the rest of the staff."

But I don't get the chance because the Filipino has gone to see "The Sound of Music" – for the forty-second time according to Greta.

"That's why he came over to this country," she says. "He associated it with the film. Sweet, isn't it?"

"Hum," I say. Actually, I quite liked the film but it's not the kind of thing you boast about to your friends, is it?

"Now," says Greta removing her wrap and throwing herself full length on the settee. "Let's have that drink we were talking about."

I don't remember us talking about a drink but maybe I was thinking of something else at the time.

"Fix me a martini, darling," she says.

I wander over to a drinks tray that looks like an aerial view of Manhatten, but there is nothing with Martini written on it. A bottle described as Noilly Prat, which does not sound very nice, and a smattering of gin, vodka and whisky but no Martini.

"How do you like it?" I ask, ever resourceful. Her eyes rake mine and I realise I might have put injured percy in jeopardy. No! It's not a kind of vaseline.

"Regularly," she says. "No. What do you recommend? I've never tangled with a real life pornographer before. What should I tell them about you?"

"Tell them I don't know how you like your martini," I say. "Now, let me see. Didn't you say something about lunch?"

"This is lunch to me. Bring the drinks over here." She pats the settee beside her and turns on full beam. Poor old thing. It is just not her lucky day. The oven cleanser is definitely going to see to that. Percy will require another few days' recuperation before he goes walkies again. I must make her a nice drink to make up for it. Now, what do you put in a Martini? Vodka and gin ring a bell so I pour in a generous slug of both. The oily prat stuff sounds a bit crude but you never know. It can't do any harm can it? Now, what else? Campari? It's a nice red colour and it should cheer her up a bit. Brandy? Definitely! Just what it needs to give it a bit of body. Not much room left in the glass now, so I pop in a bit of ice and top up with sherry. You can't beat a spot of British refinement, can you?

"You're taking a long time, darling."

"I'm mixing you something rather special," I murmur, in my best George Sanders. "it's called a Leakyteeny. You haven't lived till you've tasted one of these."

You can take that any way you like, I think, as I advance on the couch.

"My God! It's enormous," gasps Greta. "And the colour! What's in it?"

"Sip it and see," I husk. "A couple of those will put hairs on your chest."

"Just what I've always wanted," she breathes. "I wouldn't mind your hairs on my chest, though." They don't mind what they say, do they? Birds these days seem to be more forward than one of Sabrina's nipples.

"What do you think of the drink?" I say, pretending I did not hear her.

"You haven't made yourself one," she says, reproachfully, raising her glass to her lips.

"I find if I drink at lunch time I can't sleep in the afternoon."

"How terrible for you – wow!"

"Do you like it?"

She takes another sip. "You're trying to get me drunk, aren't you?"

"No, I was just trying to –"

"That's how pornographers operate, I suppose. Ply a young girl with drink and then work your filthy willies on her."

"No, really, I –"

"You don't have to play games with me." Miss Starkers rises to her feet and closes the distance between us to the thickness of a couple of skins – hers and mine.

"I wasn't playing games. I was trying to make you a drink, that's all."

Miss Starkers is not listening. One arm slides round behind my back and her fingers start fluffing up the hair at the nape of my neck. Her lips start fluffing up the set I keep underneath my nose.

"Look. You're very attractive," I say, "and normally I'd be delighted to pop round here for a glass of lunch, but today I don't feel up to it."

"Are you trying to insult me?" Greta's voice sounds like broken glass fed into a waste disposal unit.

"Nothing like that – I –"

"You lead me on and now you turn the cold shoulder."

"You're getting over-excited. Why don't you finish your drink?"

"Take your filthy drink, you pansy!" Before I can move, I get the whole lot down the front of my shirt. Beware the fury of a woman scorned, said the poet and he was dead right. They can cut up very nasty.

"You're not a pornographer. You're a phoney!"

"That's right. I'm a phonograph," I gag. "Don't you see? That's exactly what I was trying to tell you. The whole thing was a misunderstanding. Tell your readers that and you'll be doing me a big favour."

"I wouldn't tell my readers if you dived off Big Ben into a sponge," snaps Starkers. "Coming round here, acting the big shot. You should be ashamed of yourself. There's too many of your sort about now. A girl can't find a decent red-blooded man any more."

"I don't know where you get all this 'girl' nonsense from," I say. "You wouldn't see thirty again if I lent you a telescope."

"How dare you! ? Rotten little pouf!"

"If you reckon that every bloke that doesn't fancy you rotten is a pouf then I reckon you won't find many straight merchants between here and Tooting High Street," I say with dignity. "I'm not bent, I just happen to have squirted oven scourer on my old man. It takes the edge off your appetite, you know."

"Is that why you did it?"

"Not exactly. Thank you for the drink."

I shake my soaking shirt at her and open the broom cupboard.

"That's the broom cupboard," she says.

"Yes," I say. "Goodbye." I open the front door and go out. It is not one of my great exits but it gets me through the door with my trousers on.

CHAPTER SEVEN

"Well done, Lea," says Sir Ivor, patting me on the shoulder. "I don't mind admitting that I was worried about you there. That woman can be damned persuasive if she wants to get a story out of you."

"It wasn't easy," I say, keeping my upper lip stiffer than a Hashamite's hampton, "but I thought I'd better play the white man. How did you know I kept my bat straight?"

"I rang the edition of that rag she works for. She said you resisted all her blandishments."

That is all he knows, I think. If she had tried blandishments I might have weakened.

"I'm glad you came through with flying colours," continues Sir Ivor. "I have complete faith in sending you out on your first assignment now."

"And what's that, Sir?"

"Prostitution with Miss Golly."

"Blimey!"

"Yes, Lea. We believe in starting you off at the deep end. But don't worry. I think Miss Golly has a soft spot for you. Go easy with her, won't you? She's led a sheltered life and this could well be the first time she's been exposed to life in the raw. You know what I mean?" I nod. "Good man. I suggest you take her round some of your old haunts and make a few sorties on houses of ill repute. Introduce Miss Golly to some of the unfortunate inmates and let her take it from there. Have you ever run a brothel?"

"Good God no! What kind of bloke do you think I am?"

"I'm sorry, I'm sorry. It's a question of definition, I suppose. To an outsider like me, running a brothel seems no different to appearing in blue films."

I suppose I could go through the whole bit about it being an accident but somehow I don't seem to have the strength any more. Once you have flashed your nasty for posterity it is very difficult to make people believe that you can do anything else for a living.

"Good morning." The words fall from the lovely lips of Miss Helen Golly who is looking almost jaunty in her light brown herring bone suit and crocheted stockings. Unless my beady old eyes deceive me, there is a trace of self-raising flour on her cheeks – or could it be face powder? I only hope she is not going to be snatched away from me by white slavers. Who knows what effect her untainted loveliness may have on the depraved appetites of the merchants of minge?

"I've got my notebook," she says tapping a handbag that looks large enough to take a telephone directory. "Down to work at last. It's going to be jolly exciting, isn't it?"

"It should have its moments," I say. "Where would you like to start?"

An expression of strain immediately grapples with Miss Golly's features. "That's up to you. I mean, er – you are the expert, aren't you?"

"Of course. I was forgetting," I say. "Well, in that case, we'd better slope off for a cup of char. It's a bit early at the moment."

"Isn't that a good thing? Won't we stand a better chance of catching them before they – er – are –"

"On the job?" I say helpfully. "Yeah, I suppose you're right. But most of them won't have got up yet. Demand doesn't usually build up till after Tony Blackburn."

"You think there is some connection?" muses Miss G. "I have an uncle who is quite well-placed at the BBC and he may be able –"

"No, no. I think it's more straightforward than that." I say, noticing that Sir Ivor is avoiding my eyes. "Come on. Let's get out on the beat."

We catch a bus up West and push into Soho with me

trying to ignore the way locals are looking at us. "Don't carry your umbrella like that," I tell her. "We're not going to be attacked."

"It's got a sharpened ferrule," she says with quiet pride. "My grandmother gave it to me for my twenty-first birthday present."

I ignore that and sweep her in to the first snack bar we come to. This is not a very good choice as it turns out because the place stinks of rotting lino and is obviously where the blue bottles come to die. It is difficult to tell where they end and the sultanas on the buns begin.

"Do you fancy a cup of tea?" I say. "I reckon it's favourite. The coffee in these places usually tastes like warm porridge."

"Tea would be very pleasant. I wouldn't say no to one of those flakey buns, either."

"I would, if I were you. The flakes just dropped off the ceiling."

We sit and drink our tea in silence and I gaze in to her phizog and think how the landscape could be improved by having a little less foliage. She is not a bad-looking bird at all. One of those faces that grows on you. It was unkind of me to bracket her with her mate, Queen Hooter.

"You don't have an evil face," she says suddenly, leaning across the table.

"Thank you," I say. "Neither do you."

She does not know quite how to take that and we continue in silence until a couple of sharp-looking blondes come in and park their arses a few tables away from us.

"Look!" hisses Miss G. "Tarts!" I wish she did not have such a loud hiss, because the birds promptly turn round and glare towards our table.

"– and the pastry was fantastic, too, wasn't it?" I say loudly, wrinkling up my eyes in a "belt up!" gesture.

"What pastry?" says Miss Lame Brain. "I was talking about those two good-time girls over there. Why don't you go and introduce yourself?"

"Cool it!" I snap. "And for God's sake lower your voice. They look like chorus girls to me. Tell you what. You hang on here and I'll go and track down a couple of real pros and come back for you."

"You won't be long, will you?" says Miss G. grabbing her umbrella tightly. "I've heard what can happen to girls in places like this. I don't want to be incarcerated in North Africa."

"I don't blame you," I say. "I wouldn't even fancy it under the National Health. Now, wait here and I'll be back in a few minutes."

I nip outside and cock my ear for the crackle of plastic macs. A few yards up the street is a newsagents, and a lot of blokes you would not invite to start a new religion are bluebottling the small ads. "Large chest for sale." "French lessons given." "Learn to whip." "Once used rubber wear." They all sound a bit kinky to me. We don't want to shock Miss Golly too much. "Miss Pringle gives advanced driving lessons." That sounds a bit more like it. Straightforward, anyway. I make a note of the number and pad back to the Kosikomfit Kaff.

All is not well. As I go through the door, Miss Golly is against the wall with her umbrella pointing menacingly at one of the blonde jobs' bristols. That lady has a ketchup bottle in her hand and shows no signs of looking for a hot dog to shake it over.

"Mr. Lea! Mr. Lea!" pants my hard-pressed team mate in the race against filth. "Help me!"

"Is this your little boy?" sneers Blondie. "How much do you pay him for his services?"

"What seems to be the trouble, ladies?" I say civilly.

"Your lady friend asked us if we were on the game," snaps blondie's mate. "We didn't come here to be insulted."

"No need to, I imagine," I say evenly. "Come now, I'm certain there must have been some misunderstanding." I gaze hopefully into Helen's worried mug.

"I was only thinking of their welfare," says that lady weakly.

"You see. She's still at it," snarls blondie. "Miserable old dyke. Just because we're not bent we have to put up with her insults. Tell me what do you two do to each other. I'm really interested."

"What does she mean?" says Helen coming all over aghast. "Is she suggesting that –"

"Lousy old Lesbian."

"How dare you!"

"Watch it!" Blondie brings back the arm holding the ketchup bottle and a fair-sized dollop sails across the room to land on the proprietor's mush. I find this pretty funny until I get a separate serving across my denim shirt.

"Steady on girls! Ouch!" I don't know if you have ever tried to break up a fight between a bunch of women, but my advice is – don't! They have a lot of difficulty connecting with each other but anything passing within five yards stands a great chance of getting clobbered. I am no exception. First Blondie bashes me over the bridge of the nose with her ketchup bottle and then, as I blink through the tears, Helen pokes me in the goolies with her sharpened ferrule. Poor Percy! My privates must be getting a persecution mania. If only I could explain to them that they are just going through a bad patch. Helen is, at least, most apologetic.

"I'm terribly sorry," she gushes. "It must have been most awfully painful. I just saw red, that's all."

"I thought I was going to see red, as well," I tell her. "You want to be more careful with that thing. Another couple of inches and I could have been looking round for a boy soprano to start a double act."

Helen reflects for a moment. "That might be very nice," she says. "I didn't know you were musical."

"Musicians run in our family," I tell her. "They have to. Now, come on. I've found an address that might do us a bit of good. Scrape that pie filling off the front of your whatsit and let's get down to it. And, please! Restrain yourself. Think what Sir Ivor would say."

"I'm sorry." Miss Golly's eyes fill with tears. "I had no idea they came from the Living Dance Company."

"It only occurred to me when that bird kicked me in the earhole while I was still standing up. Anyway, let's try and put all that behind us. What you're going to see now may distress you, it may disgust you, but try and keep yourself under control. O.K.? Comprennez?"

Miss Golly nods meekly. "Very well. Rest assured I won't let you down again. Where are we going?"

"Miss Pringle's Advanced Driving Lessons" I tell her.

Miss Golly blinks at me. "I don't understand. Why are we going there?"

The naïveté is almost touching, isn't it? Having a bird like her on a porn commission is like asking Yul Brynner to advise on hair styling.

"They're not really advance driving lessons," I tell her. "You've got to read between the lines. It means a kind of sexual how's your father?"

"But how do you know they really aren't driving lessons?"

"You'll see." I tell her. "You'll see. You don't insert an advertisement like that round here unless you mean business. Blimey, they ought to be in smoked glass cases, some of them."

Miss Golly is gazing at me intently again. "You're not really all bad, are you?" she says thoughtfully.

"Not all bad. Right, here we are. This is the place."

"It says Advanced Driving School," says Miss G. pointing at the peeling sign in the brown-washed window.

"Of course it does. It's not going to say Brothel in coloured light bulbs, is it? There's a law against that kind of thing."

Really! She is so out of touch this girl, it is ridiculous. How she ever heard about pornography in the first place is beyond me.

"I'll do the talking," I say. "There will probably be

some kind of maid who will take us into the – you know, where it all happens."

Miss Golly nods briskly and tightens her grip on her umbrella. "I feel all keyed up," she says. "It's just like going out to play hockey for the school. Jolly exciting."

I nod and push open the door which tings a bell just like an ordinary shop. Whatever will they think of next? Inside there is a small office with a large, hairy bloke sitting behind a desk full of invoices. I suppose he must double as maid and bouncer. It probably cuts down on the overheads. The invoices are a surprise but everything is a mass of paperwork these days, isn't it?

"I've – er, we've come to see Miss Pringle," I say discretely.

"She's sick," says the bloke hardly looking up. "You'll have to have Mr. Gloshi."

"*Mr.* Gloshi?" queries Miss G. "Oh, my goodness!"

The geezer behind the desk looks up sharply. "They don't come any better," he says challengingly.

For a moment, I think Miss Golly is going to pass out. You can't really blame her, can you? I mean, I know anything goes these days, but you have to keep some kind of standards just to know where you are.

"I don't wish to know that," I say. "I'm interested in a woman."

"So am I," breathes Miss G.

"Sure it isn't just because he's an Indian?" accuses Hairy.

"That's the very least of my worries," I say firmly. "You must have some women somewhere. It says 'Miss Pringle' on the advertisements."

"She's the only one and she's sick, like I told you. Listen. If you don't like Gloshi, you can have me, if you're prepared to wait until after dinner."

"U-u-u-rh!" Miss Golly is beginning to slide towards the floor.

"Listen," I hiss. "This is a driving school, isn't it?"

"Of course it is. What did you think it was: a knocking shop?"

"Please!" I say. "Watch your language. There's a lady present."

I have to take her on to another café and get a glass of water before we can continue.

"Sorry about that," I say. "It was just one of those things. It's all a bit complicated these days. I still can't think why they put the advert in with those other ones."

"I can," sniffs Miss G. "You signed on for a course of six lessons, didn't you? They probably make a fortune out of men who are too embarrassed to confess that they made a mistake. That Miss Pringle is probably sitting on a goldmine."

"Just like some of those other birds, eh?" I say enjoying my little joke. Miss G. looks at me coldly and the smile slides off my face like it has been traced on a steamed up window pane.

"No coarseness, please," she says. "We have both acted foolishly today. Don't let us compound our mutual stupidity."

"I wouldn't want to do that," I say wondering what she is on about. "What do you want to do now?"

"Find a real prostitute," she says, so loudly that the bloke we are passing gets a crick in his neck, he turns round so fast. "Where do you find their advertisements?"

"Any newsagents round here," I say. "Look. That one for instance."

" 'Miss Lash. Stern disciplinarian'. Is that one – ?"

"Yes, yes," I hiss. "But not so loud. You're supposed to jot down the telephone numbers, not read them out like Christmas Cracker mottoes."

"Why are they couched in such violent terms?"

"I don't know. People find it kinky, I suppose."

"You mean perverted."

"In a way, yes. I suppose so."

"Don't they want normal, straightforward sexual relations?"

"I expect they get enough of that at home. I mean, it's all advertising, isn't it? They're trying to dress the whole thing up, make it larger than life, more attractive than the – er – product next door."

"It merely seems more sordid to me."

"Yeah, well –" I shrug my shoulders. It is very difficult for me to comment because I have never felt the urge to pee in a wellington boot or slip on a pair of leather y-fronts. Sometimes I think there must be something wrong with me. I never think of rubber as anything more than what you use to get the dirt marks off paper panties. I do not want to get in the act. I just want to know what it is all about. Never to have felt a twinge may mean that I am undersexed, or something.

"Let's try that one." I follow Helen's eyes and see that she is looking at "Double bed for sale". "Seems straightforward enough, doesn't it?"

"O.K. Do you want me to do the talking?"

"Why not? You were so effective last time. Don't ask me to help you carry the bed down the stairs, though."

"That was a joke, wasn't it?" I say, making a point of looking into her eyes.

"You noticed."

"Your jokes tend to stand out a bit. Come on, grab your umbrella and let's get on with it."

This time we have definitely hit the real McCoy as I sense when my nostrils bump into the smell of cheap perfume that hangs around the stairs leading to 14a. The doorbell is a plastic nipple in the middle of a plastic breast and I wink at Helen as I shove my digit against it. "See nipples and dyecast," I say.

"What?" she says.

"It doesn't matter. I was trying to see how much your sense of humour could stand."

The door is opened by an old bag who looks like Oliver Hardy in drag. In fact, I look behind her to see if Stan Laurel is there to clinch it. She is wearing a maid's costume with frilly blouse and short black skirt revealing two of the worst legs outside the elephant house at London Zoo. On second thoughts, I retract that as being unfair to the elephants. Make it outside anything. Her black stockings have more runs than a top class ski resort and the state of her pinny suggests that she has just completed an oil change on a ten-ton truck. All in all, she has the instantaneous animal appeal of Jack the Ripper with a bad head cold.

"I wonder if we could have a few minutes with – um – the lady who wishes to sell her bed," I hear myself saying.

"You can have a few hours with her if you've got the ready," says Maid Gruesome. "She's a bit tied up at the moment, so you'll have to wait." For some reason best known to herself the hideous crone starts to laugh. "Did you hear that?" she chortles. "'A bit tied up at the moment'. Ooh – er, I'll be the death of myself, I will really."

Just at that moment there is a heavy crashing noise from next door almost simultaneous with a scream of pain. "Excuse me. Make yourselves comfortable." The maid shoots through the door and both Helen and myself crane our necks after her. Lying trussed up on the floor is a large naked woman whilst a man dressed in a frogman's suit with mask and flippers is staring up at a rope hanging from a pulley fixed to the ceiling. The door closes before we can catch more than a glimpse.

"Incredible!" gasps Helen. "What have we stumbled across? Shall I fetch a policeman?" Before I can answer, the maid pops out again.

"Are either of you any good at tying knots?" she says. "Reef knots, preferably."

"I haven't tied a serious knot since I was a Brownie but – no, wait a minute. On second thoughts I don't think –"

"Neither do I," I say firmly, shaking my head.

"Oh dear. Are you quite sure?"

"Positive."

The maid goes into the bedroom again and I sit down with a copy of "Popular mechanics". "What's happening in there?" hisses Mrs. Golly's pride and joy. "Don't you think we should tell someone?"

"I don't think anyone, apart from them, is going to be very interested," I say.

I am just getting engrossed in how to make a tea trolley that turns into a drying frame at the drop of a few screws, when the bedroom door opens and a red-faced geezer comes out wearing a black jacket, waistcoat and pinstripe trousers. He is carrying a bowler hat, umbrella and brief-case and there is a red mark round his mush where the rubber mask must have pressed into his flesh.

"Uncle Edgar!"

The poor basket nearly drops his copy of the Financial Times as Helen comes up with the big hello.

"Helen, m'dear. What a surprise. How's your dear mother? Keeping well, I hope. Must dash. Lot of things to do. Having a bit of trouble with my back. Massage, don't y'know. Works wonders. Must look us up next time you're in town. Give m'regards to the family. Must keep in touch. Toodle Pip." He hardly stops for breath as he backs out of the door threatening to put his bowler hat on and then dropping it down to waist level as if to protect his goolies.

"Ho, ho," I say. "Uncle Edgar is a bit of a lad, isn't he? I bet your aunt doesn't know he slips up here for a spot of massage."

"I can't believe it," gasps Helen, threatening another attack of the vapours. "I haven't felt so mortified since mummy told me about making babies."

"Yes. It does come as a bit of a shock, doesn't it?" I say, trying to comfort her. "I was quite relieved really, because I always thought you did it with your belly button and could never understand why I never had an erection."

Miss Golly winces. "Quite," she says, clipping the word off as if with a pastry shaper. She is obviously most put out by naughty Uncle Edgar and I am wondering whether we should draw a veil over an unhappy morning and break for an early lunch when the maid reappears.

"Right," she says. "Ten pounds please."

"Ten Nicker! I'm not paying your old age pension as well, you know."

"No need to be offensive!" snaps the crone. "There are two of you."

"We don't want to do anything," I explain. "We just want to ask the lady a few questions."

"Yeah. I've heard that before," sniffs Shagnasty. "We get your sort on the blower all the time."

"I am merely interested in her modus operandi," says Helen severely.

"What you do once you get in there is your own affair," says the old bag disdainfully. "But you don't get across that threshold until you cough up ten quid."

This conversation does not seem likely to get us anywhere not costing a ten nicker entrance fee, and I am not sorry when a large lady appears through the bedroom door, massaging her wrists. She is wearing a black negligee that does such a lousy job covering her knockers that it is more like a negligent. As for her makeup, it looks like the colour register on a cheap comic. For a moment, I think she has four eyes.

"Do I hear voices being raised?" she says sounding surprisingly refined. "That's about all anybody seems to be able to get up these days, without 'extras' "

She smiles at me and then turns her attention to Helen. "My God!"

"Cynthia Gottno-Nixon!"

"Helen Golly! Good heavens! Fancy seeing you here. On the other hand, I suppose it's the perfect place for an old girls' reunion."

"Cynthia was head girl of St. Sennapods," says Helen not without a trace of pride. "And Captain of hockey. Cynthia, what brings you to this?"

"My Rolls usually," says Big C breezily. "But sometimes I take the Jensen if I feel like driving myself. Money, darling! A desire to wallow in ill-gotten gains. You remember how much loot everybody seemed to have at St. Sennapods? I became absolutely determined that my shoulder was going to feel the caress of mink and, after my A level results, this was about the only way left, apart from marriage, and I was never grade one matrimonial material. Big in the withers, that's what Miss Gartshore used to say. Do you remember her? Hateful old harridan! She was absolutely beastly to me."

"But Cynthia, isn't it awful having all those strange men doing things to you?"

"Most of them never touch me, darling. Look, if we're going to talk, let's pop into my room and do it over a drop of gin, shall we?"

She sweeps back into the inner room and waves a hand at a pile of debris in the middle of the carpet.

"Excuse the squalor darlings, but these buildings are on their last legs. There's hardly a wall you can fix a block and tackle to. Poor Mr. Pamfret nearly fell on his harpoon gun. It could have been very nasty."

"He was my uncle," says Helen.

"Thought I'd seen him before," says Cynthia, enthusiastically. "He used to try and look up one's knickers during the gym display on Founders Day, didn't he? What a small world it is."

"I still don't know how you can do it," shudders Helen, as the maid comes in with three large gin and tonics.

"Darling, like I said, one has to do so little these days. One needs a gymnasium rather than a boudoir. Straightforward sex is the last thing that is in any of their minds. I don't think I've had to perform the act since last Thursday, and that was with a Persian who hadn't been over here very long."

I must say, looking round the room, I can see what she is getting at. Whips, masks, boots of all shapes and sizes, rubber suits – even an old gas mask as worn by my dad when he saved Britain from the Third Reich. I wonder if he left it here? It could have been just the kind of place he would have done most of his fire watching from.

"Nevertheless, I would never have thought that you had it in you."

"That's just what I'm saying, dear. Very seldom. I think it may have something to do with my particular body type of course. Being, well – shall I say Junoesque?"

I nod. Why shouldn't she? It's a free country. "I attract a lot of small men. They seem to want to be dominated. They're quite sweet some of them. They jump up and down like little dogs."

"Were you influenced by pornography when you took up your – er profession?" asks Helen gulping clumsily at her gin and tonic.

"Not particularly, darling. It was the money mostly, like I said. Of course, those books that used to circulate at school helped make the whole proposition not seem too unutterably boring. You remember? What was that one you used to have? 'Passion's Pasha' wasn't it?"

Miss Helen Golly turns the colour of posh shithouse paper. "What book? You must be mixing me up with someone else."

"Darling. Don't be so coy. I remember you sitting in the corner of the dorm devouring it like secret tuck."

"It was utterly harmless," says Helen. "It didn't have photographs like some of them." She shudders.

"Oh yes! Do you remember those ones that Francesca Cringe found under the butler's pillow? I never really quite understood what she was doing in his room anyway. You remember how she left very suddenly in the spring term? Her father used to be one of my best clients. I was terribly upset when he had his accident. Still, it was ridiculous dressing up in a suit of armour at his age. All that weight, with his heart. And standing in those gold fish bowls, too. He was the only man I knew with rusty toes. Not surprising he got a chill on his wedding anniversary."

"Not at all," slurs Helen. I notice she puts down her glass very unsteadily and is obviously not used to the half potty of gin that gay, fun-loving Cynthia dishes out. I, too, am beginning to feel the old sloe-juice tickling my toes and both Cynthia and Helen suddenly begin to look decidedly fanciable. I sense that I could fall deeply in love – well, six inches anyway – with either of them given half a chance. Fortunately this moment comes faster than a weak-willed wop in a warm room.

"I think I know what you're here for," says Cynthia coyly. "We get a lot like you."

"Pornography Commission?"

"No! People who get an extra thrill out of making love in a tart's bed."

"Really!" explodes Helen. "You don't –"

"Darling! Don't worry about it. It's nothing unusual. You should hear some of the requests I get. Actually, it fits in rather well with my plans. I've got to have lunch with a Client today. You can have the run of the place."

"Cynthia. Please understand –"

"Don't thank me. It's quite all right. I know you'd do the same for me. What was the old St. Sennapods motto? 'Do unto others as they would do unto you, but do it first!?' Something like that, anyway. I am sorry I can't spend more time with you but Sir Gawayne is rather special."

"Sir Gawayne!?" Helen's eyebrows threaten to scrape the ceiling. "Not Sir Gawayne Greenknight?"

"Gentil and parfait as they come – which is not without a hell of a lot of trouble sometimes. Why? Do you know him?"

"He's my step-father." Helen looks as if she has just found out that Father Christmas is a child molester. "But I don't understand. He's confined to a wheelchair."

"That's right," sings out Cynthia cheerily. "Blossom. Bring in some more gin and my adjustable spanner, oil can and goggles."

"He seemed such a nice old man," sighs Helen.

"He is. He is. An absolute poppet," says Cynthia stepping out of her gown and revealing the flesh banquet beneath. "Excuse me changing in front of you like this but I'm a little behind this morning."

She bends down to straighten her stocking seams and I would tend to disagree with her. From behind she looks like two kids fighting under a blanket. Blossom brings in some more booze and Helen gulps it down like she is in a state of shock and has just been given a glass of water. Miss Gottno-Nixon clambers into a slinky silk number and starts buttoning up.

"Don't worry about money," she says. "If you feel like leaving anything there's a box outside for the 'Distressed Gentlefolks' Association'. All contributions gratefully received. Shall I tell Gawayne that I bumped into you?"

"What? Oh, no! Don't mention it. I don't want him to know what I'm doing at the moment."

"Probably just as well, darling. It's often the naughtiest ones who can be the most easily shocked, isn't it? Look, angel, I must dash. Lovely to see you again. Do keep in touch. I keep meaning to go back to the old place but you know what it's like. Things do seem to get on top of one, don't they?"

Hardly have I had time to agree with her and say ta for the booze than she is gone, closing the bedroom door behind her. Helen tries to get to her feet but she is obviously finding it difficult to remember whether she is coming or going. Faced with the two alternatives I have a clear idea which one I would choose and settle down swiftly to attain my end – or get my end away, as they say in some circles. Helen has now become indescribably lovely and I cannot imagine how I have kept my hands off her for so long. Her skin glistens temptingly like the outside of a well-bred steak and kidney pudding and I watch eagerly as her dainty fingers flush the bottom half of her gin and tonic past her tonsils.

"I can't believe it," she says. "Cynthia and Uncle Edgar and – and –Dadsy wadsy."

"It's a funny world," I murmur sitting beside her on the bed, whence she has conveniently alighted. "You'd be amazed at some of the things that go in – I mean – on."

She nods her head slowly. "It makes me ask myself if it's all worthwhile."

"Exactly," I say, my voice thick as peanut butter spread by a two-year-old child with a shoe horn. "Everybody else is enjoying herself, why not you?" I lean towards her lug-hole and drop my hand on her thigh. She examines it like it is a star fish.

"I know," she breathes. "Oh dear, I do feel funny." I stretch out my right hand to make contact with one of her knockers and am therefore in an ideal position to disagree with her.

"You don't feel funny to me," I say tenderly.

"You mustn't. You shouldn't . . ."

Her voice dies away smothered by my friendly lips. I press her back against the pillow, which smells like homage to Boots perfume counter, and stretch myself out beside her. Her eyes are closed which I reckon indicates that she does not want to feel involved in what is going to happen to her, and instinctively my hand glides up underneath her tweed skirt. It is not a texture I am particularly used to but then it is pretty unusual to find a bird not wearing trousers these days. I do not like that because you have to have very long arms to be able to stick your mitt up from turn-up level and if you start unzipping their flies you feel as if you are touching up a fellow. Maybe I am over-sensitive, but that has always been my trouble.

One bonus with Helen is that she is not wearing tights. I always find them very unhealthy especially for one's circulation – I mean, that elastic can cut into your wrists something cruel, can't it? The moment my eager pandy touches naked thigh, I feel as if I have been plugged into an electric circuit. Currents of desperate lust flood through my version of Ted Heath's favourite instrument and my mouth leaps into action again. I have never kissed a bird with a moustache before and it is not bad really. Like eating crispy noddles through a cheese grater.

"What are you doing?" she says.

"I'm trying to take your knickers off with one hand," I tell her. "I'm not doing it very well, am I?"

"I don't know. I have no one to compare you with," says Helen. "Oh, goodness! This is awful. I shouldn't just be lying here."

"True," I say. "But don't worry about it. You need a bit of practice before you can start making a useful contribution."

She gives a sort of shudder and covers her face with her hands while I remove her panties, stockings and suspender belt and tug down her skirt.

"I'll never be able to look Sir Ivor in the flies – I mean, the eyes – again," she sighs. "I must be mad."

"You're not mad," I say. "This is the sanest thing you ever did in your life." Well, I suppose that could be considered a bit of an exaggeration, but a girl needs reassurance at a moment like this, doesn't she?

"Is it going to hurt?" she asks plaintively.

"I'll try not to scream," I say bravely.

"I didn't mean you!" she snaps.

"Have you done much riding?" I ask her. On the evidence of my fingers she must have brought in a couple of Derby winners.

"I used to go in for a lot of gymkhanas," she says.

"Jim Khan's what?!" I ask her. These Paki blokes are no slouches when it comes to business and I believe in keeping in touch.

"Horse gymkhanas," she says. "And hacking of course."

"That's probably why you were hoarse," I say. "I used to suffer from chest colds a lot when I was a child."

"I don't know what you're talking about," she says. "In fact, I hardly know what's happening. I feel – hey! What are you – oh. Oh! Oh!!!"

I have come over so torrid it is horrid and Percy has disappeared like a python into a rat hole – O.K. would you believe an enthusiastic viper? This girl must have done a lot of gripping with her knees because she holds me tight as an outside-in batting glove and I feel myself vibrating like a piece of fluff at the mouth of a suction cleaner.

"Oh!" she groans. "Oh! Oh! Oh!" She digs her fingers into the small of my back and suddenly I begin to feel that I am losing control of the situation. "Ah!" she gasps, hungrily. "A-rrgh!!"

"Hey! Hang on a minute," I say talking to myself, but it is too late. Helen Golly starts vibrating like a shit-house door in a hurricane and I am taken out of myself so completely that I can almost hear Percy uttering a hoarse croak. It happens so quickly that I do not have a chance to think of hobnail boots, Hughie Green's bicycle clips or any of the other things that normally stop me boiling over. H.G. thunders on for a few moments and then it dawns on her that something fundamental has changed between us.

"Have you finished?" she says.

The note of surprise and disappointment in her voice is something I know I am going to carry with me to the grave – if I live that long.

CHAPTER EIGHT

"Miss Golly speaks most highly of you," says Sir Ivor, patting me on the back. "You gave her invaluable succour."

I feel myself blushing down to the roots of my short and curlies. How did he know that? I did not reckon on Helen being one of those birds who shoots her mouth off about every detail.

"Something like that," I mutter.

"It must have been a harrowing experience for a simple country girl. We must be careful with her."

You've left it a bit late, I think to myself. What are you on about, you stupid old rat bag?

"I think she'll be able to cope, Sir," I say. "She buckled down to it with a willy – I mean will."

"Capital, capital. Her stepfather is a very close friend, you know."

"No, really?"

"Yes. Tragic about his accident."

"What happened?"

"Swan-upping."

Blimey! I have heard that swans can turn a bit nasty and it is not surprising, is it? I thought there was a law against that kind of thing. Probably is, unless you are a toff. The upper classes get away with murder. Fancy having a mate like that and being allowed to become president of a Committee investigating pornography? I have half a mind to write to the R.S.P.C.A. about it. Wait a minute! I heard that! Who said I have half a mind, period?

"I have been thinking that we might embark on a joint activity," murmurs Sir Ivor resting his hand lightly on my shoulder.

"Oh, yes." My voice bears out the suspicion I now feel when any of the Committee come near me.

"Yes, Lea. I have been much agitated of late by the profusion of low-class drinking clubs that are springing up all over the West End. They offer striptease of a particularly lewd and offensive nature and in some cases the girls who work there are actually prostitutes."

He makes it sound so attractive. I wonder if they issue season tickets.

"You want to visit some of these places?" I say.

"Frankly, the prospect appalls me," says Sir Ivor snootily. "But I fear we would not be doing the job we set out to do unless we put in an appearance. I am convinced that the entertainment provided corrupts and depraves the customers, to say nothing of the deleterious effect it must have on the entertainers themselves."

"Have you anywhere in mind?" I ask.

"Yes. There is a particularly repulsively named establishment that has just opened called 'The Strip-Strop Leather Fanciers' Club'. I believe it would repay a visit."

"With the girls and Professor Joddrell?"

"I think that by going in a party we may be able to protect ourselves, in some measure, against the incursions of those unfortunate females whose unhappy lot it is to work there. Of course, you probably have first hand experience of any number of these places. I should have asked for your advice. My apologies."

Just as well you did not, I think to myself. The nearest I ever got to a strip show was when Aunty Aida had a few too many at Edna Bangle's coming out party – she had just come out of Holloway. I remember mum was very cut up about it, as was the tablecloth Aunt Aida used for her dance of the seven veils. Mum always said she was the wild one of the family. She had been on the halls in her youth and on the booze ever since. I remember her well because she was the last woman in Britain to be run over by a tram – blind drunk of course. She used to get letters about it from tram enthusiasts and opened a scrap book which was a great comfort to her in her declining years.

I am still thinking about Aunty Aida when Sir Ivor's Rolls purrs to a halt outside the "Strip-Strop Club". The bloke on the door has eyes that dart round his mug like blobs of mercury and I bet he can see a copper round three corners. The streets in this part of Soho are flat dustbins and Amanda starts playing up the minute one of her pumps collides with a scrag end of very elderly meat.

"Oh, it's awful," she says.

"You mean offal," I say, showing her what a little laugh riot I can be.

"Really!"

"Timothy's made a joke," says Helen who has become meltingly attentive since our visit to Cynthia Gottno-Nixon. "It's all to do with meat, isn't it? You see 'offal' means bits of animal's insides, doesn't it? And you said 'awful' so –"

"I understand his feeble joke," snarls Amanda. "Oh, look at that! It's disgusting!" I watch her peepers glaze over as she grabs a butchers at the photographs outside the Club. Very big girls they are, and not risking heat stroke some of them. "All that flesh exposed to the lewd, lustful eyes of sex-sated men," hisses Amanda, the drool practically dripping from her lips. "People should be flogged for taking photographs like that. They should be tied to a whipping post and the shirts torn from their glistening sweat-soaked backs. As they twist and squirm –"

"Yes, yes, my dear Miss Pumps," says Sir Ivor hurriedly, before Amanda goes into orbit. "I'm certain we all share your concern about this revolting trade. Now, let's go and size up the enemy."

"I'm sorry," says Amanda. "I don't know what came over me."

"Must have been very easily aroused, whatever it was," says the doorman unkindly. "Yes ladies and gentlemen. Don't miss the show of the century. And I do mean show. You'd see less if you was married to them. Six beautiful girls from around the world demonstrate ancient lovecrafts that have been handed down from mother to daughter since times immoral. If you're not broad-minded don't bother to come in."

"Do you do teas?" says Helen.

"Only striptease," says the doorman. "Let me see. Five of you at two guineas with V.A.T., P.A.Y.E. and cover charge. That's twenty-seven pounds nine and eightpence or in this new money: Thirty-two pounds exactly."

"That's disgusting," says Sir Ivor.

"Exactly! What do you think you're paying thirty-two pounds for? I'm amazed they haven't closed this place down. I hardly like to look at the show myself."

"Oh, pay the ghastly little man his money and let's go in," says Amanda. "If we have to wallow in brute depravity, thrust ourselves into a maelstrom of writhing, thrashing bodies. Flinch and quiver before the –"

"Thirty-two pounds did you say?" says Sir Ivor plunging his mitt into his wallet.

"That's right, guv – you won't regret a penny of it. It'll give you more ideas than a Do-It Yourself manual." Marble-Eyes turns to me and winks. "He looks as if he's been doing it himself manually for years, doesn't he? Poor old sod. It's a shame, really."

I nod and Sir Ivor bustles us through the curtained entrance into the dark and smokey interior. It is difficult to see anything and the first face I focus on is that of Ferret-Features who took Sir Ivor's cash a couple of seconds before. This gentleman is now seated behind a table with a roll of tickets on it. He smiles evilly. With a face like that, there is no other way for him to smile.

"Good afternoon," he says. "How many? Five? That will be eighteen pounds including service."

"What!?" shrieks Sir Ivor. "We just paid thirty two pounds."

"That was for membership," says the doorman indignantly. "Officially I'm bending the rules to let you in before your credentials have been verified."

"I had that done when I was a child," says Hans

Joddrell seriously. "My mother was a slave to genital cleanliness."

"Shut up, you fool!" snaps Sir Ivor. "Now. What the hell is this about eighteen pounds?"

"Entrance charge!" says Ferret-Features. "You don't expect to get in for nothing, do you?"

"I don't call thirty two pounds nothing!"

"I keep telling you. That's the membership. We have to charge that to keep the place exclusive. We don't want undesirables getting in, do we?"

"It's iniquitous!" storms Sir Ivor.

"You watch your language mate. If you don't like it you'd better talk to the owner. Mr. Noggett!"

Almost before my ear-holes can become attuned to the familiar name and my hand check that my wallet is still in place, Sidney appears before us. He is wearing a dinner jacket with lapels so narrow they look like braid and a frilly pink shirt. He looks like Tom Jones with middle-aged spread.

"What's the trouble, Reggie?" he says, and then he recognises me. "Timmo! What a turn up. You've given those porn-broker berks the slip, have you? Hang on a minute, and I'll be right with you." He turns to Sir Ivor and party. "Yes, gents, what can I do for you?"

"I'm with them," I say hurriedly. "This is Sir Ivor Bigun and some more of the – er – the Committee."

"*The* Committee?" says Sidney and the colour of his face begins to make the whole room lighter.

"Yes," I say, gazing into his minces meaningfully. "*The* Committee."

"Hold on a minute, gents," says Sid and he grabs my arm and drags me into the gents – well it smells like the gents. "Have they come to make trouble?" he groans. "Blimey. Just my bleeding luck. This place was going like a bomb, too. Could they get it closed down?"

"Relax, Sidney," I tell him. "Pull yourself together. Don't talk to me about bad luck. I'm the one who's in the nick, remember. I'm only out on parole."

"Oh, stop whining," bleats Sid. "You're always coming out with that bleeding heart stuff. Give it a rest for gawd's sake. There's plenty of openings here for you when you come out."

"So I was hearing, Sid. And not just one by all accounts. Your friend Reggie was telling us what an exciting show it was."

"Stupid blabbermouth! I'll shut his cakehole for him." Sid shows what a joy he is to work for.

"He was only trying to do his best for you Sidney. Fifty quid for five people isn't bad going."

"Half of that will have gone in his back pocket. You can't trust them, you know. Oh, my gawd. What am I going to do with Ivor Whopper and his mates? This show is bluer than gorgonzola. If they start getting nasty I could be ruined."

"Tell them to tone it down a bit."

"Then what are the customers going to say? They're not going to like that, are they?"

"Bugger the customers, Sid. It's only one house. You won't have Sir Ivor and his mob here all the time. If you give a few of them their money back and tell the others to belt up you should be all right."

"Yeah." I can see Sidney's evil little mind churning over the alternatives. "Yeah. You may have a good point there. O.K. I'll go and talk to the girls. Try and hold your lot up a bit, will you?"

But when I get back "my lot" have paid up and pushed on into the auditorium. Apparently the light was so bad in the foyer that some dozey git mistook Amanda for a woman and tried to touch her up.

"His hands were everywhere," she gasps. "Touching, rending, exploring, imploring. The brute sinews straining against my outraged flesh. Like a helpless doe I –"

"Yes, yes," says Sir Ivor. "It must have been exceptionally unpleasant for you. But, look on the bright side. Does this not bear out our worst fears concerning the effect these sinks of depravity can have on people? Who knows what we have yet to see?"

Everybody shudders except Professor Joddrell who adjusts his specs and shoves his hands deep into the pockets of his mac.

We are standing in a low ceilinged cellar full of bald-headed, middle-aged men who look as if they are waiting for an auction to start. Considering how many of them there are, and how close they are standing to each other, it is amazing how their eyes never seem to meet. At one end of the cellar is a small stage surrounded by peeling coloured lights and at the other a bar. Behind the counter is a bird with an afro haircut and enough make-up to paint the Mona Lisa on the side of St. Paul's Cathedral. Her eyelashes hang over her peepers like foliage weighted down with black snow and her knockers must have been used as barrage balloons during the last war. They are about as natural as Ted Heath's smile and even less tempting.

"Yeh, gorgeous," she says, catching my eye. "Do you fancy a drink?"

I look towards my companions, but they all pretend they have not heard, except Helen who shakes her head shyly.

"I'll have a brown ale, thanks luv," I say deciding that they can all get stuffed.

"We don't have a licence, dear. It's coke or a fruit juice cocktail."

"Fruit juice cocktail?"

"You can have it fortified." She attempts a wink which makes her look as if she has suddenly sprouted a black eye. "Do you want to try it?"

Something about the way she wriggles her tits makes me think she is not only talking about the fruit juice cocktail.

"O.K. I'll try anything once."

She pours something out of a jug and adds a slug of

something else from a can – yes, a can! "Here we are. That will be one-twenty-five."

"One-twenty-five? You mean one pound twenty-five?"

"I gave you a double, and that's including service."

"Service?! By the cringe!" I raise the glass to my lips. "Blimey! What's in this? Anti-freeze?"

For a moment the bird's eyes light up in surprise. "Ooh," she said. "Nobody's ever noticed that before."

"They don't have Sidney Noggett as a brother-in-law," I tell her. "My dad used to think the stuff was vodka. Sid gave him a bottle every Christmas regular as heart failure."

Further discussion concerning the recipe of the Strip-Strop Fruit Cocktail has to be abandoned as the lights go down and the audience surges forward towards the stage. A tinkle of broken glass and a scream of pain suggests that someone has found it. The unshattered bulbs go on and a grimmy of near nausea proportions is revealed standing in the middle of the stage. She is wearing a football shirt and wellington boots. If it was not for the bird's face I would say the act had possibilities, but she is so plain as to be able to walk through an Italian prisoner-of-war camp unmolested.

"Disgusting!" hisses Amanda and for once I agree with her. The record player is bashing out "Sherry je t'aime", which I had always thought was the alcoholics' national anthem, but suddenly this disappears with the needle still on it to be replaced by "In an English Country Garden". The bird on stage gazes helplessly towards the wings and seems unable to move.

"Come on darling! Let's see something," shouts one of the audience and the rest are not slow to support his view. "Get 'em orf!" "Drop 'em!" they howl.

It is into this threatening situation that Sid launches himself like the old pro he is.

"Right!" he says bursting on to the stage. "We need a little help for this act. Any volunteers? You sir? Marvellous! And you, and you – steady on! Don't all rush at once. One at a time, please. Yes. Now, you sir. Take your jacket off please. Excellent. Now your waistcoat. Now, Monika, put them on please. Very good. Let's give the gentleman a big hand for being such a good sport. Now, you sir. Off with your jacket please. Monika – put it on –"

In no time, all the blokes on the stage have removed articles of clobber and Monika has put the lot on. The only bit of flesh you can see is the tip of her hooter – horrible it is, too.

"I don't understand," says Helen. "What are they doing, Timothy?"

"Looks very harmless to me," I say loyally.

"It can't be harmless," snaps Amanda. "It must have some obscene connotation. Dressing up instead of undressing in a place like this – it's unnatural."

Unfortunately, most of the customers seem to agree with her.

"Stop messing about!" "Get on with it!" "Git 'em orf!" The shouts of protest give way to a slow hand clap.

"Gentlemen, please!" says Sid desperately. "Surely there must be another sportsman amongst you? All we need is an overcoat and Monika need never catch cold again."

"I don't care if her tits freeze solid," shouts a thick-set geezer in front of us. "I didn't come here to see a bleeding fashion show."

"That's right, mate, you tell him."

"Get your knickers off!"

With that masterly sense of timing which has saved him from disaster so many times, Sid realises that the time has come to move on to the next act.

"Fantastic, Monika. Fantastic. Well done, darling, that was marvellous. I'm certain you'd all like to show your appreciation of a wonderful –"

Sid checks as a penny hits him just under the eye.

"And now for an act of rare skill and breast-taking – I mean breathtaking – beauty. Carmelita and her erotic – I mean exotic – tassle dance!"

"Disgusting!" says Amanda hopefully.

"I am most interested in the reversal manifestation," muses Joddrell. "Never before have I seen the clothes on the woman going. It was quite remarkable. Almost beautiful in fact. A spontaneous act of life-enhancing charity that transcended the mundane sterility of the stereotyped sexual ritual."

"You took the words right out of my mouth," I say. "I wonder what we're going to see now?"

"A couple of yards of knocker whirling round like a wind machine, I hope," pants the watery-eyed weirdo feeling for his handkerchief beside me – at least, I hope that is what he is feeling for.

"How awful!" sighs Amanda.

But she is wrong again. When Carmelita comes on to the stage she is wearing an ankle length overcoat.

"Oh blimey!" snarls the bloke next to me. "This is beyond a joke. I got more kicks out of watching the Russian women's team march past at the last Olympics."

"Where are the tassles, mate?"

Sidney stops another handful of small change and dives his mitt into his pocket. Delivering a cheerful thumbs up sign – at least I think he intends to use his thumb – he starts fastening a couple of tassles to the breast buttons of Carmelita's overcoat.

Immediately a chorus of groans and whistles fills the air and the sound of the Sabre Dance being played with a rusty knitting needle is almost drowned in expressions of intense frustration and disappointment. Carmelita starts revolving the upper part of her body bravely but one of the tassles gets caught in the neck of the overcoat and the total effect reminds me of somebody trying to shake off an insect they don't want to touch with their bare hands.

"I want my coat back!"

"I want my bleeding money back!"

"It's a con!"

"Do 'em!"

It had not occurred to me that Carmelita's overcoat belonged to a member of the audience but this is clearly the case. A number of disgruntled patrons struggle on to the stage in order to retrieve their property donated during the previous act.

"Nobody on stage, please!" Sidney struggles bravely but is quickly pushed to one side. I glance round and Ferret-Features can be seen shoving the contents of a bulging cash box into an inside pocket.

"Somebody's nicked my wallet!"

Oh dear! The gentleman standing on the edge of the stage turning his jacket pockets inside out looks mean as cold sunlight on a cut-throat razor. Biff! – or if you prefer it – bonk! Sidney's face always seems to get in the way at moments like that. He staggers back and almost immediately the stage becomes a mass of struggling, punching men. Rip! The sound of fabric being torn tells me that my worst fears have been realised. Yes. Amanda has torn somebody's trousers off.

"Lea!" hisses Sir Ivor. "You've had experience of this kind of situation. What do we do now?"

"Run like hell," I say, making for the stairs. "Come on! Follow me!"

CHAPTER NINE

"Ruined!" says Sid bitterly. "Ruined!"

"Come off it, Sid. With the cash that place is bringing in, it won't take you five minutes to repair the damage. And, now that bloke has dropped proceedings, I can't see what you're worried about."

"It was all your bleeding fault, as usual," sniffs Sid. "Bringing that lot here. Nutty as a fruitcake, that bird was. Did you see the nail marks on that poor sod's back? It took three blokes to pull her off him and then she says she was assaulted. I don't know."

"She is a bit funny," I agree with him.

"'A bit funny'! She's stark staring bonkers, mate. You want to watch her when the full moon comes out. I'd get a bit of barbed wire round your y-fronts if I was you. How much longer are you going on with this caper?"

"We've got to go to Denmark in a few days," I say, trying to sound very blazer about it.

"Denmark!? You jammy bastard. What are you doing there?"

"Sir Ivor reckons it's the home of filth and Hans Joddrell – he's on the committee – comes from there so we're going to see how the Danes have made out without any censorship."

"Blooming heck! You mean all those books and films and live shows?"

"Yeah. I expect so," I say, smothering a yawn.

"They need me on that. I mean, with my experience of running a club and all that. If they reckon you know something about pornography, they ought –"

"Sorry Sidney," I interrupt coldly. "You have to be in the nick before they reckon you know anything about pornography, and you didn't fancy that, remember?"

"You're still bearing a grudge about that, aren't you?

Amazing after all this time. You help to burn down my club –"

"'Burn down'?"

"Yeah. Don't you ever read the newspapers? That's what I'm on about. While you're scarpering some geezer manages to start a fire. The whole building went up. I'm in dead schtuck. You can't have a cellar without any floors above it, you know."

"No, Sid. I'm sorry. When we came there, I never knew you owned the place."

"Thanks for being sorry. Some of my neighbours are cutting up very nasty about it. They're influential people, a lot of them. Ooh. I wish I could get my hands on the bleeder who started that fire!"

"It could have been an accident, Sid."

"Yeah, I thought about that. I reckon that two-timing tea leaf Reg was using lighter fuel instead of anti-freeze in the fruit cup."

"No. It was anti-freeze, Sid. I'd swear that was the stuff you used to give dad – till he had his attack."

"I should have kept giving it to him, miserable old basket."

When Sid is in a bad mood everybody suffers and I am not sorry when he slouches off to see his insurance people. He must be a diabolical risk by now, because I can remember a few thousand Japanese vacuum cleaners going up in flames not so very long ago.

The flight to Copenhagen is uneventful. Hans Joddrell reads a book entitled "The Environmental Approach To Sub-radical Counter-culture". Amanda and Helen look out of the windows and I watch the stewardess's pantie line every time she bends over. I have always had this thing about Air Stewardesses – in fact I have always had this thing, period – but especially about stewardesses. In fact, I have even bought a book called "The Stewardesses" by one Penny Sutton. In this, a gay, fun-loving sky moppett explains what my dream fodder gets up to when they are on the job – if you know what I mean. "Prurient" is what Amanda calls it but I am not certain that I agree with her. Not until I look up "prurient" in a dictionary, that is. Sir Ivor passes the journey writing out his report in long hand and there is no doubt that a lot of writing has been done by everybody on the Committee except me. I am merely an introduction to the underworld, it seems, with little more to do than act as interpreter occasionally. Sometimes I reckon I am only there as a gimmick, and this feeling is backed up by the news that the Committee's findings are going to be made public at a press conference to be held in Penhurst Prison. At least, I will not have to go far to get home afterwards.

We get to our hotel about tea-time where we are introduced to Professor Joddrell's assistant Upför Grabbs. This bloke is as thin as Ted Heath's re-election prospects and looks as if he is trying to hold an ice-cube in his mouth without melting it. He nods bleakly to each of us in turn and informs us that a tour has been arranged.

"An Eye-full tour, I expect," I say waiting for everybody to fall about laughing. Not a sausage. Really, these anti-porn people have no sense of humour.

"First to the bookshops, we will be going," says Upför seriously. "If you wish to buy anything I will be able to get it for you at trade prices."

"I suppose it may be necessary to take some examples home," sniffs Sir Ivor.

"Better be on the safe side," I say trying to keep the eagerness out of my voice. That stuff in our hallstand is getting very old hat for me now. It will give Dad a lift, too, if anything can.

"I think this is going to be quite, quite ghastly," says Amanda. "All those sweaty, writhing bodies locked together in sexual congress. I can imagine the obscenely large –"

"Yes, yes. I'm certain you can," interrupts Sir Ivor peevishly. "May I suggest you try and keep that very fertile imagination in check until we actually get to our first destination?"

I can see that Sir Ivor is becoming a bit choked with Amanda and I don't really blame him. After the incident in the Strip-Strop Club, Amanda Pumps is revealed as a dead liability to any serious filth fighters.

Upför Grabbs has laid on a car and we all pile in with Helen snuggling down beside me. Her bedroom is next to mine, and the expression on her face as she was shown into it was, I think, intended to make me register this fact. God knows what effect the events of the next few hours will have on her.

It is not difficult to recognise the first bookshop we stop at because it has "SEX BOOKS" written in three-foot-high, scarlet letters above the covered windows. Keyhole shaped openings allow pedestrians to have a butchers at the goodies but serious browsers have to enter. This we do and are immediately greeted by a kindly-faced, middle-aged man, wearing a white jacket.

"English?" he says immediately. "I thought so. We have many visitors from Perfidious Albion."

I imagine he is talking about one of those fourth division football teams, though why they should all come here, I don't know. Still, I suppose they have to take what friendlies they can get. Sir Ivor looks embarrassed. "We're here on business," he says stiffly. "Our interest is purely professional."

"You wish to be our agents in Blighty?" says the bloke in the white coat. "I hear that things are much easier over there now. Come into the back room and we can talk about it over a glass of aquavit."

Fortunately Hans Joddrell springs forward to sort things out and we are left to our own devices – or vices as seems more nearly the case. "If you want any special perversions, come and see me," says our friend helpfully.

All round the room are counters strewn with books and magazines all neatly labelled according to subject matter. "Whipping", "Rubber Wear", "Leather". It does not escape my notice that English seems to be the first language used in every case.

"Disgusting!" says Amanda picking up a book entitled "Mr. Whippy, I Scream".

"Yes, the reproduction is not good," says the shopkeeper apologetically. "I have it on fine art paper if you would prefer it."

I must say the reproduction in some of the other books leaves nothing to be desired. In fact, that is the trouble with it. By the time I have skimmed through half a dozen magazines I feel I have been looking at a "Woman's Own" supplement on how to judge cuts of meat. And why do they always have pimples and wear socks? I know I go on about socks, but I do feel strongly about it. Maybe it is just me. Maybe I am the only bloke in the world who does not find naked men in socks hugely percy-provoking. All over Western Europe blokes are probably striding into bedrooms with nothing on but a pair of Wolsey Griptops and birds are going spare. In the darkest jungle clearings dusky gentlemen with bones through their hooters are sliding on a pair of deodorised terylene/wool mixture reinforced-heel, ankle-length socklets and the palm trees are shaking at the thought of the sexual carnage to come. Is there something wrong with me? Am I –

"Do you get a lot of young people here?" says Sir Ivor to the shopkeeper.

"Young people!? Yes, on the far counter. Of course, we do not have them too young. The authorities are very strict on–"

"I don't mean that," interrupts Sir Ivor, turning scarlet. "I mean do young people come here?"

"We discourage it. Hygiene, you know. Of course, what they do when they get the books home is –"

"It doesn't matter!" says Sir Ivor, his voice showing signs of breaking. "Look." He turns to us. "Have you seen enough? I don't think there's much point in staying here any longer. It becomes like flogging a dead horse after a while."

"Flogging a dead whore?" says White Jacket, pricking up his ears. "We have a very nice series of a live whore being flogged, but not a dead one. Maybe if you tried our other branch."

"You misunderstand the gentleman," says Upför Grabbs seriously. "He is interested in horses."

"Oh, I understand. Horses and whores. Yes we have many such pictures. Horses, donkeys, alsatians, pigs –"

"Oh, this is terrible!" gasps Amanda. "I think I'm going to black out."

"You like black men?" says White Coat. "I thought so. I can always tell. Come over here. We have one of the largest selections in Copenhagen. And when I say large –"

"You swine!" hisses Amanda. "Do you think I want to look at photographs of heavily muscled, glistening black bodies flexing their rippling pectorals as they thrust their throbbing –"

"Let me out!" screams Sir Ivor. "I can't stand it. I can't take any more!" He shambles through the door leading to the street.

"I am very surprised if we do not have something to suit his tastes. No perversion has ever beaten us before." White Jacket seems genuinely choked.

"We'd better go with him, hadn't we?" says Helen. "We're all supposed to stick together."

Before our helpful friend can make anything of that we file out into the street. All except Amanda who follows on a few moments later zipping up her enormous handbag with difficulty. Sir Ivor is leaning against the car with his elbows resting on the roof and his hands over his face.

"You would like to visit some more bookshops?" says Upför helpfully. Sir Ivor holds up a restraining hand. "No. No. I think I have seen enough. What's next on the itinerary?"

Upför looks at his watch. "I think it best that we return to the hotel and visit the Live Show after an early dinner."

"A Live Show!" Amanda shudders gratefully. "You mean we are actually going to be exposed to the disgusting spectacle of a naked man and woman locked together in sexual congress? Their heaving –"

"Miss Pumps. Please!!!" says Ivor wearily. "For the last time, I beg you to control your imagination. It threatens to engulf us all."

"I was only trying to express –"

"Please!! Not another word!!"

Sir Ivor is obviously approaching breaking point and Amanda gets the message and relapses into a sulky silence. Outside, night falls faster than a pair of concrete knickers and it is darker than an Armenian's armpit by the time we get back to the hotel. I leg it for my bedroom and am just about to step into a steaming bath when there is a gentle tap on my door. Quick to interpret the significance of this signal, I drape a towel around myself and open the door. Standing there wearing a dressing gown and a generous helping of perfume is Helen Golly.

"Can I come in?" she says. Since, she is standing behind me when she says it I feel it would be unkind to say no.

"What's the trouble?" I say, noticing that her face foliage has disappeared and that she has lost a few pounds in all the right places – or all the wrong places depending on which way you look at it.

"Those pictures," she says. "Oh, Timothy. I'm afraid I found some of them – how shall I put it? – rather jolly. Quite sexy-making, in fact. I feel I should resign from the Committee. What do you think I should do?"

"Just wait till I turn the tap off and I'll show you," I say.

So, of course, we get down to supper twenty minutes late and Sir Ivor looks at us as if he has just inspected a microfilm of what took place on the bathroom mat.

"Glad you could join us," he says sarcastically. "I thought you were never going to come."

"That's just what I thought," says Helen gazing moodily into my eyes. Astute readers will realise that I have made a big effort to correct any impression of an over-excitable nature that may have lingered on from our first bout of in-and-out.

I turn down the smoked salmon – well, it is practically

raw, isn't it? – and ask for some of the tinned stuff, but they don't have any. Typical! These continental hotels will have to pull up their socks with us in the Common Market, I can tell you.

"Where are we going after supper?" I ask Hans Joddrell, gently removing Helen's probing fingers from my thigh.

"To the Friendly Pussy Club. I think you will find it most – er –"

"Disgusting!" snorts Amanda, spraying food all over everybody.

"Yes – disgusting. But also, interesting."

He is dead right there. It is one of the interesting evenings at the theatre I can remember. Yes, it is a theatre. At least, there is a stage in the shape of a circular bed in the middle of a room surrounded by chairs. Behind the stage is a cinema screen and on to it a film is being projected as we check in our coats and enter the Club. I am not usually one for second features, but this movie has first, second, third, fourth, fifth and – I lose count after a while – features. The story line is definitely weak but for acrobatic, muff-diving, dongler-dousing and straightforward percy-pummelling it is in a class by itself. I cannot take my eyes off the screen which is maybe why I sit down on three different people's laps before I find an empty seat. Amanda is equally unfortunate, although she manages to turn every nudge into an attempted rape. It is the nearest she will ever get, poor old thing.

After a while, my eyes begin to get accustomed to the gloom and as the heroine of the film goes down for the third time – and she is not drowning, believe me – I look around to see what the rest of the audience is like. Most of them are middle-aged to elderly and remind me of the normal turn-out in a hotel T.V. lounge. I do not know quite what I had expected, but it was something more obviously depraved, I think. This bunch of serious, soberly-dressed men, plus a few women, could be watching a documentary on soil erosion in East Anglia. Not a flicker of ill-concealed lust plays around their firmly closed mouths. Only Amanda is already beginning to make grunting noises. She is a dead liability that bird; I can see what Sir Ivor is worried about. The film reaches its climax at the same time as the main character and the lights go up as a tall blonde lady steps forward to address us. She says something in Danish – though it may have been Serbo Croat – and expresses the hope that we will all be spiritually uplifted by what we are about to see. I think this is asking a lot, looking round the audience, but it is nice to know that somebody cares. We all clap when she belts up, anyway.

Sir Ivor is slumped deep in his chair with his hand over his face and thus, presumably, misses the first act. This is performed by two ladies with very large appendix scars, although I do not think that these have anything to do with their particular problem, which seems to be one of frustration and is solved by the discovery of an electric vibrator beneath one of the pillows on the bed. I would have thought that if you had an electric vibrator under your pillow you would know about it, but maybe it was planted there. Anyway, the girls seem very pleased to find it and go through a phase of delirious excitement into one of experimentation which draws from Amanda her most chilling response yet – silence.

After this we have another film which is about Girl Guides – well, the girls are dressed up as Girl Guides – at least, at the beginning of the film they are. I prefer the films because we watch them in the dark. I don't mind watching anything as long as I don't have people watching me watching it. The minute the whole thing becomes mass entertainment I want to cop out.

"Oh, Timothy, I'm beginning to get those feelings," breathes a voice from the darkness. "They're awful." No prizes for guessing who that belongs to; but let's make a short list, anyway. Yup, you were all right. Miss Helen Golly appears against Number One on two hundred and fifty thousand of the ballot papers I have just been handed.

"Relax," I say. "The night is young, and I'll hear your excuses later."

"But, Timothy –"

"No butts, no gouging, no hitting on the break. I want a good, clean fight and may the breast –"

"Oh, Timothy . . ." The girl has obviously become a wanton, and a want un to boot. Fortunately, for the sake of the Danish equivalent of E.Q.U.I.T.Y., the lights go up shortly before I have to, and the mistress of ceremonies takes the stage – and she darn near could, too, believe me. She is a big girl, that one. She does her Danish Bacon commercial and then addresses us in English.

"Up to now we hope very much that you have enjoyed our show, and that you respond in the right spirit. Now we give you our finale with the hopes that it will inspire you to bring like harmonies into your own existence."

Immediately, the sound system starts to grind out Ravel's Bolero – I remember it from "Two Way Family Favourites" – and the cloakroom attendant steps on to the stage. For a bloke who has taken so many hats and coats it is a surprise to see him stark, bollock naked but I realise what is about to happen when Lady Chatterbox suddenly steps to the rear and collides with his brute masculinity. Before you can say "Danish Back-on" the lady is stripped to the buff and they are going at each other like a couple of puppies trying to find their way round a bone.

"U-u-u-rh!!" I have never heard a water buffalo uttering its mating call, but I imagine the sound flooding from Amanda Pumps' throat cannot be totally dissimilar. Before I can attempt to restrain her a small, round object thuds against one of my eye-balls and I sink back into my chair with only the pressure of Helen Golly's hand against my inside leg measurement for comfort.

The small round object is one of the buttons that Amanda is shedding as she rips her clothes off. "Filthy animals!" she screams. "Disgusting! Depraved! Debased! Despoiled! Desirable!! Delicious! Delectable!!! Hey! Wait for me! Amanda wants it!"

My eye is watering so much that I cannot see anything but I can hear her voice going into orbit. All around me is the sound of breaking furniture and passionate grunting and groaning. Somewhere a man is crying. That must be Sir Ivor. Poor old sod. Eager fingers tear open my flies and I am pressed back into the wreckage.

"Poor darling," breathes Helen. "Don't worry. Mumsy will kiss it better for you."

CHAPTER TEN

"Spinach," says the Governor "that's what it is, spinach." He is a new Governor and very old school tie and jolly. Mr. Firm is still in the intensive care unit.

"It doesn't taste like spinach to me" says Helen. "What do you think Timothy?"

We are being entertained to dinner in the posh dining room at Penhurst prior to the important press conference at which the Fight Unclean Culture Korps report is being presented to a battery of newsmen. "We" are Sir Ivor, Professor Joddrell, Helen, Amanda and myself. Amanda has a black eye and I must say I think it improves her. That Danish boy certainly put up a tremendous fight for his honour. Too bad he was giving away so much weight.

"I don't know" I say, "I never ate much spinach as a kid. I was afraid of ending up with a bird like Olive Oil." She is right though, it does taste funny. I can see the others giving it a few old-fashioned glances.

"Comes from the prison gardens y'know," says the Governor, "amazing the amount these chaps have produced. I'm not surprised our young friend here isn't enthusiastic."

I smile sociably and look round the table. I hardly recognise them now that they are tarted up in their best bib and tucker. When I think back to the scene as the police broke in to the Friendly Pussy Club I can hardly believe that I was in the company of the same group of people. For a start, I always thought that Hans Joddrell wore something under his long trench coat. And as for Amanda! Well, really! How she managed to get the hat-check boy in that position I will never know. I have seen nothing like it since the last World Sumo Championships. No wonder Sir Ivor had to be carried to the police ambulance. Not that I was in the best position to see because by the time my eye had stopped watering Helen had thought up a very effective way of obscuring my vision. It is the late developers you want to watch, you know. Some of these birds try and cram ten years missed experience in to some very unusual places.

Thank God Sir Ivor was able to pull strings at a very high level otherwise we might still be in that Danish clink. I have nothing against smörgasbörd but I prefer to sleep under normal sheets and blankets if given a choice. I think they had to get Dame Margot Fonteyn over there in the end to sort it out. Not in person, mind, but with The Royal Ballet. Her and The London Philharmonic in some kind of reciprocal cultural exchange. We got a bloke who messed about with puppets and appeared on Jackanory.

Anyway, we got out which is the main thing. Thank Goodness the Danes are a broad-minded people, as they said themselves.

I thought that would be the end of it. I mean you cannot imagine coming out of that lot with your y-fronts over your arm and sitting down to write a report about the dangers of pornography, can you? But they do. Every man jackass of them. The minute we get back to Blighty they are all scribbling away like there is a prize for the first one to finish.

Only Hans Joddrell seems to be prepared to take the broad view, and when you think of the view of that broad he was getting behind the counter this is hardly surprising. Helen wavers a bit, but then she has that kind of body. She says that she is worried by the way she feels about me. I am worried too, and I have asked her to stop feeling me in public. Helen's attitude is typically feminine: "stop it, I like it". If you get a kick out of something, it must be bad for you. Other people should be protected from having feelings like yours because they might not be able to control them. Control! Faced with the prospect of nooky that baby shows less control than a two year old at the wheel of a runaway truck. If you don't believe me ask my mother – no, don't ask my mother. I told her I caught my jeans on a barbed wire fence.

Mum and Dad and Sid and Rosie have all been invited along to see what Sir Ivor calls my "redemption". I feel like someone who has just made the last payment on a hire purchase agreement. Rosie is "indisposed", but I reckon she does not want to risk bumping into Daisy Deacon's old man. If their friendship was platonic then my name is Roger Carpenter.

Mum has a few words with me before dinner – she only has a few words, poor old thing – and it is clear that she now reckons me almost as highly as when I was on the brink of becoming a telly personality. That is what I like about Mum: you can't keep her down for long. If the house fell down she would start building a rockery from the rubble thirty seconds after the dust had settled.

"Don't forget to speak up and sound the ends of your words, dear," she says.

"I'm not saying anything, Mum. I'm just sitting there. Sir Ivor is doing all the talking."

"Well, mind you sit up straight, then. Ooh, I feel quite excited. Don't you, Father?"

"No" says Dad. "It's not likely to be the happiest day in a father's life, is it? Visiting his son in the nick. When I think of how I sweated and slaved, scrimped and toiled –"

"Tote that barge, lift that bail,
Pissed all night and he lands in gaol"

sings Sid. "Come off it, Dad. We'll all be blubbing our eyes out if you don't give over."

Just at that moment an old screw I have not seen before comes over. "All right, you," he says. "Back to your cell. You're not supposed to be out till the Press get here."

"I happen to have been invited to luncheon with the Governor" I say witheringly.

"I know that," snarls the screw, "I meant him."

"Him! ?" The screw is pointing at Dad.

"Yes, you, Crusher. You came in with the last intake, didn't you?"

"What are you on about! ?" screeches Dad. "You're mixing me up with someone else."

"Oh, no I'm not, 178345 Crusher Lea, isn't it? I remember you at Parkhurst." One glance at Dad's ashen mug is enough – for a lifetime in most cases.

"Hello, hello, hello," says Sid. "You never told us about that then, did you? I always thought he had shifty eyes. Get him in the right light and there's quite a look of Crippen about him."

Now I can see why Dad gets his knickers in a twist every time I have a little brush with the 'bules. He sees himself in me all over again. Fascinating, isn't it? O.K. So you've had enough of Clement Freud. See if I care.

"This man may be my father, but he has payed his debt to society," I say nobly. "Unhand him."

The screw does not look as if he thinks this is a very good idea and it is fortunate that a warder is passing who can confirm that Dad is only a temporary visitor. Fortunate for Dad that is. For his wife and family it is a blooming tragedy.

"Crusher!" says Sid. "Blimey, what did you crush, bath salts?"

"I only slipped from grace once," moans Dad, "and I have to put up with this."

"I remember her," says Sid. "She used to hang about outside the Bricklayers Arms, didn't she? Big girl. I'm not surprised you had problems."

"Shut your mouth, you coarse basket!" snarls Dad. "You know what I meant."

"What were you in for?" I ask.

"About thirty seconds, by the sound of it," says Sid unkindly. He can be very crude sometimes.

Dad does not take very warmly to that remark and it is a few blue moments before I can ask my question again.

"It was during the war," he says grudgingly. "Other people were prepared to foresake their wives and families but I knew where my duty lay."

"So you deserted?" says Sid.

Dad chooses to ignore this unworthy slur. "Like I said, I stayed at home to look after you and your mother."

"I never saw him except when he ran out of coupons," says Mum.

"He was doing the pools, was he?" asks Sid.

"Don't be daft. I mean ration coupons. Food was rationed then, wasn't it?"

"Don't look at me, I wasn't Prime Minister."

"Do they put you in the nick for deserting?" I ask.

"I had to forage," says Dad with dignity.

"The Red Caps were after him, you see," says Mum.

"You mean he deserted from Butlins?" says Sid. "Blimey! That's punishable by death, isn't it?"

"Red Caps not Red Coats, you berk. Mum's talking about the military police, aren't you mum?"

"Yes dear. They were always round the house trying to trace your father's whereabouts."

"It had probably slipped out again," says Sid. "He can't have been able to get his iron pills."

"Give over Sid," I tell him. "I want to hear how Dad landed in the nick."

"I was trying to make sure you had enough to eat," says Dad, his voice charged with emotion and over-acting. "I stole some eggs."

"And they sent you to Parkhurst? Blimey, that's diabolical. I know there was a war on but –"

"Forty-two thousand eggs," says Mum.

"Forty-two thousand?!"

"The whole quota for an egg-processing plant."

"The children had to eat," says Dad.

"Yes Dad, but forty-two thousand eggs! We'd all be roosting on the mantelpiece by now if we'd eaten that lot."

"Who were you going to flog them to?" asks Sid.

"'Flog them'? I wasn't thinking about flogging them. I might have exchanged a few for bananas."

"What happened to them?"

"He panicked and tried to flush them down the khasi," says Mum.

"That's why they call him Crusher, is it?" says Sid. "Should have been Flusher, shouldn't it?"

"'Sabotaging the war effort'. That's what they said he was doing. The neighbours wanted to string him up."

"They haven't changed much, have they?" says Sid.

"I was only thinking of the kids," grunts Dad.

"Gets you right here, doesn't he?" says Sid pointing to the pit of his stomach.

Dad is very quiet after that and I can't help feeling sorry for the poor old sod. I can just see him crunching up all those eggs and trying to force them round the bend. It must have looked like an Australian christening party.

"More spinach?" says the Governor, interrupting my thoughts. "Might as well enjoy the fruits of your labours, what?"

"I never did much work in the gardens" I say. "I hardly know what the stuff looks like."

"Well I do," says Amanda, "and if this is spinach then I'm a sex maniac." She gives a funny little giggle when she says that. Not like her at all. Very strange.

No sooner am I out of the dining room than Fran Warren comes bounding up to me like an old English sheep dog. He is obviously glad to see me.

"Back to the fold," he chortles. "Ooh, I am glad to see you. You've no idea how lonely I've been since you went away. There's nobody here I've got anything in common with."

I wish he would not say things like that. Especially when people like Arthur Ian Legend and his side-kick, Grass, are about.

"Touching reconciliation," sneers Legend. "At least it will be if we leave them alone for a couple of minutes."

"Did you have a nice dinner?" asks Grass. "Did the

Governor say who had been nicking the spinach?"

"He must have been. We had some for dinner."

Legend and Grass stare at each other and then back to me like they are trying to read some secret written on my face.

"Did you have much?" says Grass anxiously.

Blimey! They are mean baskets, aren't they? They must have flogged tons of the stuff and they are worrying about the piddling little amount we noshed.

"Not enough to disrupt production," I say sarcastically.

"That's all you know," says Legend, looking as worried as Ted Heath studying the balance of payment figures. "This could be very nasty. Do you feel anything?"

"It's too early" says Grass.

"What are you blokes on about?" I ask. "There's nothing wrong with the spinach, is there?"

"Of course not," says Legend hurriedly. "No, it's just that it's a special strain. Got a lot of iron in it, it takes a bit of getting used to."

"Everybody had some, did they?" asks Grass.

"Yes."

"Oh my gawd!"

"Right. You lot. Get moving!" It is the turn of the screw to interrupt us again. "You're wanted on stage, Lea. The rest of you, file down to the hall."

"I didn't think we were allowed to have files."

"Shut up! I don't want any of your lip."

"Are you lot coming to watch?" I ask.

"Oh yes. I wouldn't miss this for anything," says Legend, raising his eyes towards the ceiling.

"Good luck," trills Fran. "I'll keep my legs crossed for you."

"This month's special offer," says Legend as they go off down the corridor.

The hall is laid out with a long table on the platform at one end, and the committee range along it facing an audience of newspaper-men in the front few rows backed by my fellow prisoners. I can see Mum, Dad and Sid in the third row. Mum gives a little wave.

"They're undressing me with their eyes," hisses Amanda. Again she gives that funny giggle. What has come over the woman?

Helen is sitting next to me on the other side and I find myself gazing at her lips. I have seen them many times before but now I am studying them as if they had an independent existence. Every line and moulding seems to be so large. Her lips are giant satin pillows on which I wish to lay my head. It is only as I am leaning towards her that I suddenly snap out of it as if awaking from a dream.

"I feel strange," she says, taking the words out of my cakehole. Before I can say anything Sir Ivor stands up.

Then sits down.

Then stands up again. "Ladies and Gentlemen," he says. "First of all, I would like to thank you all for being here today."

"I didn't have any bleeding alternative, mate," says a voice from the back of the hall.

"Thank you," says Sir Ivor. "Now we all know why we're here."

"No, mate. What are you in for?"

"Sex and filth," continues Sir Ivor, speaking as if half asleep, "are threatening to undermine the very fabric of our society. Unless we do something about it we run the risk of suffering the same fate that overtook the Roman Empire."

"You mean bingo on Thursdays and Saturdays?"

"I refer, of course, to the erosion of moral and spiritual values leading to the collapse of the state. If we are going to avoid the holocaust, then I believe we must suppress the dissemination of books like these –" he indicates a pile of the magazines that the customs officer found in Amanda's suitcase "– full of pictures of girls with big squidgy titties."

Do my ears deceive me? And what about that funny giggle? It must be the spinach.

"You said it, Stud," exclaims Amanda, leaping to her feet. "Let's have some action. I've got a couple of big 'uns, too." The last few words are muffled because she is pulling her jumper over her head.

"Tidal wave of filth," muses Sir Ivor. "You can't take a Whitehouse anywhere."

"Oh, Timmy, I've got those feelings again," whispers Helen passionately. "Only worse."

Sir Ivor has now sat down and is staring intently at one of the magazines. Amanda has got her sweater off and is standing on the table and wriggling out of her skirt. Hans Joddrell is – no! he can't be! Not here. Not in front of all these people. Oh, dear! What was in that spinach? Somebody must have drugged it. Hey! Wait a minute. I look down in to the audience and there is Grass. Grass. I always thought they called him that because he had green fingers but – of course! Grass means pot, doesn't it? And not the kind you piss into. Cannabis. Legend and his lads have been flogging pot, grown on the prison premises, and we have just knocked back a couple of platefuls.

It must be that, mustn't it? I mean, I would not normally be carrying on like this. I can hear the audience cheering and above it all my mother's voice shouting something, but I just don't care.

"It's a bit crowded on the table, isn't it?" says Helen.

She is right. Amanda takes up a lot of room wherever she goes. I wonder how much they will add to my sentence for doing this? About fifteen years I should think. Still, I will be in with a very nice class of person. I feel really good now. All warm and relaxed. Totally committed to one end: my own.

"Oh, Timmy, Timmy, come on, I can't wait."

"Hang on a minute," I say, "I must get my socks off."